RUBY: DRAGONSLAYER

J E THOMPSON

ARC BOOK CLUB, LLC

ISBN: 978-1-952677-10-6 (Paperback)

ISBN: 978-1-952677-04-5 (eBook)

For my wife and best friend, Wallis.

BLURRY

She woke to the steady dripping of water onto the filthy stone floor.

A flickering light danced in the corner of her vision, and she blinked blearily against the darkness of her surroundings. Her gaze focused on the lonely candle in the corner of the room, and she watched as its low flame wavered gently in the still air.

Droplets of water fell from the ceiling and threatened to extinguish the only source of light in the cramped prison cell. When she slowly turned her head, she could see the dull glint of the solid metal bars that held her captive.

Everything hurt. She lay on her back, and the sorry excuse of a mattress was the only barrier between her and the cold stone floor. Concrete walls loomed on the other sides of her cell, and a faint shuffling from behind one of them told her that she wasn't the only one imprisoned in this place.

Ruby.

That was her name. For some inexplicable reason, she was sure of it.

Her mind sharpened, and she grasped at the elusive memories that seemed to be just out of reach. Memories of her past, of anything she held dear...they had all disappeared.

After a few futile attempts to remember how she had come to be captured, she slowly rolled to her side, groaning as her sore muscles protested against every movement. At the very least, she knew that she hadn't been here for her entire life. Somehow, she knew what sunlight was. She knew how grass felt under her bare feet. She could practically feel the wind caressing her cheeks.

As Ruby reminisced, she began to ache to see a sunrise, a sunset...anything outside of the four walls of the dingy prison.

When she tried to speak, to demand her whereabouts, only the faintest of whispers came out of her dry throat. Ruby coughed violently, hacking up dust and what looked like old blood. Swiping the back of her grimy hand against her mouth, she noticed two metal bowls by the bars of her cell. One was filled to the brim with filthy water, and the other held a strange gray sludge.

Ruby's stomach roiled at the thought of consuming either of them, but she knew that any sustenance was better than none at all. Closing her eyes, she drank the water quickly. Too quickly, she noted, as she retched and did her best to keep it down. She coughed again before pinching her nose and bringing the other bowl to her lips. It smelled sour, like bread that had been left to mold, but she consumed it slowly, knowing that she would need her strength to escape.

"Hello?" she called out softly. Her voice was thin and raspy, but it worked.

Someone grunted. Others stayed quiet or shuffled their feet, but no one answered her. She crawled unsteadily to the bars of her cell and tried to peer at the prisoner across from her, but there was only darkness.

Ruby collapsed against the cold metal bars and dragged herself into a sitting position before casting a critical eye over her body. Her hands were covered in grime, and her fingernails were nearly black. She touched her hair and winced as her fingers met the greasy and knotted strands.

"Please, someone," she croaked. "I need to know how long I've been here."

"Shut it," someone growled. Ruby pushed herself away from the bars as the others grunted in agreement, returning to her cot and decided that it was probably best to stay in the shadows.

Everything was a mystery. Ruby hated idle speculation, but her thoughts were her only companion here. She chose an undisturbed corner of the room and drew a thin line in the dust, marking a day.

Her only hope was to get information out of a guard the next time one of them brought her food. But the next day came and went, and no one arrived. Clearly, the prisoners were fed every other day, if even that. Indignation warred with anger inside of her, and she ruthlessly tamped down her emotions, choosing instead to try speaking with the other prisoners again.

"Tell me what's going on, and I'll be quiet," she demanded the first night, when she thought she heard whispering. The moment she spoke, the whispers stopped, and she sighed in frustration.

On the second day, she tried again. "Why don't they bring us food every day?"

"If I could get out of this cell," the same man who'd snarled at her said, "I would strangle you to death, little girl."

"You'd waste your freedom on me?" she retorted.

"It wouldn't be a waste to kill you, so I suggest that you stop asking questions before your voice becomes too familiar, and I know exactly who you are when I get out."

Discouraged, she stopped trying to speak to the others, though she still heard the occasional whispered conversations. Ruby yearned for something, anything, to ease the monotonous boredom of staring at the walls of her cell.

On the third day, a guard finally came. His heavy footsteps clanked down a stairway that didn't sound far from Ruby's cell. She excitedly pressed her face against the bars and tried her best to get a good look at the man.

It was impossible. The large man was outfitted in heavy armor and wore a helmet that completely covered his face. Ruby almost didn't speak when the man pushed her bowls through the bars, but at the last moment, just before the guard turned away, she did.

"How long have I been here?" she asked quietly, but loud enough that the guard looked down at her. She could feel his eyes on her from under his sturdy helmet, but after a moment, he dismissed her and turned to walk away.

"Hey!" she called. "Answer me!"

She threw her body against the bars, rattling them loudly and ignoring the prisoners yelling at her to keep quiet.

The guard simply turned and stared at her in silence before turning away again.

"I will let them know you are awake."

That small acknowledgment was enough for Ruby, though she didn't know whether that was a good or bad thing. Her thoughts took a familiar path, and she couldn't help but wonder if they were going to kill her. But still, she could not understand why they took her memories, if all they wanted to do was to get rid of her.

Even so, she knew why her memories were gone. Magic. Everyone had a past. Everyone started somewhere, and Ruby was absolutely certain that she did not start in prison. She frowned and closed her eyes, willing herself to remember, to overcome the magic that locked away her memories.

It was useless. The harder she tried to remember, the more it felt like there was an invisible barrier in her mind that kept her from accessing her memories. It felt as if she peered into a foggy mirror...she could barely make out the shapes, the colors...but the harder she tried to reach them, the fainter the images became.

Ruby waited what felt like all day and all night. Clearly, she'd caught the attention of someone who was much higher ranked than a simple prison guard, and she couldn't help but wonder why. Perhaps she was a hero in a world of villains, or she was a long-lost princess kidnapped by an enemy.

Though her hypothetical situations were comparatively amusing and helped her pass the time, they also highlighted the direness of her situation. She was trapped for an unknown reason, with little to no information about any aspect of her imprisonment.

Hours later, she heard footsteps—two guards, maybe, and a third person with much lighter footsteps. None of them clanked in the same way the guard before had, though.

The door squeaked open, and a blinding light flooded the room. Ruby stifled a shocked yelp and covered her eyes with her arm.

"Oh! Sorry, I forgot you were all used to the dark," a man said with a tinge of amusement.

Something squeaked, and the light grew dimmer. When Ruby opened her eyes, she saw that he carried a lantern with a small gear at the base that could be turned to adjust the light.

The man himself was a strange sight. Tall and lanky, he was dressed in a lush robe of deep purple that looked far too big for his body. Underneath, he wore brown and white, and she instinctively knew that all three colors combined meant that he was a nobleman. Two burly guards stood behind him, partially concealed in the shadows.

A small part of Ruby hoped they were her rescue party, but with each passing moment, the likelihood of that happening grew smaller and smaller.

Ruby didn't say anything as the man stooped down and examined her closely. His piercing blue eyes roved over her, and she fought the urge to shrink beneath his gaze.

"So, you're the one, hmm?" he asked, more to himself than to Ruby. She just nodded, and the man tilted his head at the guards. "Get over here with some of that food and water."

They did as he asked and pushed more bowls through the bars. Ruby eyed them curiously and was shocked to see that they weren't full of the same sludge, but real food. The tantalizing aromas of chicken and asparagus wafted over to where she sat on her mattress.

She looked up at the robed man. "Are you here to rescue me? Or is this a trick?"

He laughed. "Somewhere in the middle, I would say. Now, eat up. You have a very long day ahead of you tomorrow, little miss assassin."

"What?" Ruby asked, but the man stood up and retreated toward the door without a backward glance. "Assassin," she murmured, and a snort sounded in the darkness.

"You know the law, don't you?" another prisoner jeered. "Murderers always face execution without question. That's how it's always been in Torbek."

Ruby remained silent. Torbek must be the kingdom she was in. Somehow it didn't seem like it was her home, though she couldn't say for sure. Instead she focused on the nobleman's words.

He'd called her an assassin. That accusation rang through her mind for the rest of the night, even as she savored the food she had been given. She ate slowly, unashamedly licking her fingers clean before deciding against licking the bowl as well.

The nobleman hadn't given any indication that she was to be executed.

In fact, he had even said that his intentions were somewhere between a trick and a rescue, though she had no idea what that meant. What she knew for certain, though, was that her sentence or execution depended on the details of her crime.

Who had she killed? How did she kill them?

An endless river of questions and a suffocating fear of the unknown plagued her, though with a full belly, she quickly drifted into a restless slumber. Dreams of death and decay tortured her unconscious mind. She must have died a hundred times, burning in pits of fire to desperately running from swarms of vicious rats.

Ruby woke with a start. The tattered rags she wore were drenched in sweat.

"I see you're a little nervous."

Ruby turned her head toward the voice. The nobleman was back, dressed in another luxurious purple robe.

"Do I die today?" she asked, careful to keep her voice neutral.

"Well, that's up to you."

Ruby's eye twitched at the man's intentional vagueness.

"Why am I here?" she pressed. "You called me an assassin."

"A few evenings ago, you assaulted and murdered a member of the King's Court. Upon being taken down and brought here, you suffered a concussion. The concussion caused your memory loss, it should be temporary."

"I killed someone?" Ruby asked incredulously. She didn't know why, but the very thought was incomprehensible to her.

"Yes, you did. It was a grievous crime, particularly from a foreigner such as yourself. Seeing as you are not of this kingdom, you were given no leniency whatsoever."

7

"So, I'm going to die," Ruby said, clenching her hands.

"As I said, that depends entirely on you."

The man smiled as if he wanted to say more, but seemed content to wait until Ruby cracked.

She huffed in exasperation. "What's my punishment, then?"

"I'm so glad you asked," he beamed at her before tapping his chin thoughtfully.

Ruby rolled her eyes, not fooled by his theatrics.

"Witnesses described your agility and combat prowess with a strange, sickening type of admiration. You were elusive with the guards as well, and it took considerable time and quite a bit of force to subdue you, hence your concussion and memory loss."

The way the man spoke with such delight about her supposed abilities raised Ruby's suspicions.

"As such, we cannot allow you back on the streets—you could ruin the fragile, little kingdom of Torbek. Your punishment will be possible death."

"Explain what that means!" Ruby snapped, impatient. Clearly, he enjoyed taunting her.

His smile widened at her outburst. "You will face two challenges. Failure in either one will result in your death. Success will result in banishment, but you would be allowed to live."

"Could you explain the challenges, then?" Ruby tried to quell her rising annoyance.

"I could."

"Go on." Ruby glared.

"First, you will face a trial by combat. Your opponent will be a very angry half-orc who murdered an innocent innkeeper and his family! You two committed a crime of similar weight, and only one of you will be allowed to live."

Ruby frowned. "And the second one?"

"Well, you'll only get to that challenge if you win."

"What is it?"

"You will see in time…or, perhaps, you won't. I hope that will be enough motivation for you to win. I would say that I prefer you to a very angry, very murderous, very desperate creature."

Ruby raised an eyebrow. "And you think that I can win solely off of my curiosity?"

The man laughed. "Oh, of course not!"

He pressed the back of his hand to his cheek as though he was telling her a secret. "Truth be told, I don't think you can win at all, but I suppose we'll just have to see, won't we?"

Ruby crossed her arms over her chest to ease the trembling in her limbs. She bit down any question about why she had been given a chance for a stay of execution. After all, she had no idea how things were done in Torbek. "When do I fight the orc?"

"Half-orc, actually."

"Fine, when do I fight the half-orc?"

"In exactly two hours. My men have brought you more food, so eat up and prepare yourself for the bloodiest day of your life! Or, maybe, the second bloodiest. It *is* funny, isn't it? If not for the drop of human blood in the half-orc's veins, he wouldn't have even had a trial, and you'd be fighting someone a little easier to beat. Ah, the world is fateful sometimes, maybe you were meant to die."

Before Ruby could formulate a response, the man gave her one last look before turning and walking away. From the shadows, two men emerged and gave her more food. It smelled heavenly, and she all but salivated.

"You want to share some of that?" the previously hostile prisoner asked sheepishly.

She laughed loudly. "You're a fool," she spat. "Maybe you should have been a little more helpful."

"But I'm not the one dying today."

Ruby ignored him and took her time eating everything she'd been brought. The spices were delicious and familiar, though Ruby couldn't name them—she was almost certain that they had come from this kingdom…though she couldn't remember the kingdom's name either.

The man had said her memory loss was a result of a concussion, but she didn't believe him, nor did she believe that she had killed someone. The thought of senselessly ending another person's life turned her stomach, but she thought ahead to the half-orc. Ruby knew herself. She would fight tooth and nail to stay alive, even if it meant killing another being.

Despite her decisive reasoning, she hesitated. She wanted to think of the half-orc as a murderer, but in the slim chance that the nobleman was right, and she *was* a murderer…

Ruby continued eating, frowning as thoughts of good and evil warred in her mind. If she *had* killed someone, she couldn't imagine a scenario where she wouldn't have had a good reason. Though, of course, simply having a reason didn't mean her actions would be justified.

She placed the empty bowl by the bars and rose to her feet. There was at least another hour left before her fight.

Ruby eased into a defensive stance, breathing deeply and ignoring the beads of sweat that started to build on her forehead. As she easily flowed through a sequence of punches and kicks, she couldn't help but think that her body was too practiced, too familiar with battle.

She shook her head and cleared her mind. There was no time to waste on useless thoughts.

SOMETHING DEADLIER

As the minutes ticked by, Ruby felt a strange coil of excitement tighten in her belly. Her body was prepared to fight, though the realization was foreign and shocking. She couldn't recall ever fighting anything orc-related, but she had already known that her amnesia stole most of her memories.

Though the thought was incomprehensible to her, she realized that fighting had always cleared her head. It was like an elegant dance that she had memorized and perfected—energy flowed over her body like water, and she tucked herself away in the deep recesses of her mind.

Ruby exhaled, calmly focusing on what she could remember after waking up in the cell. There was darkness, but there were also flashes of half-buried memories. Snippets of a journey, of guards forcing her down into the prison.

The stain of blood on her hands.

Gasping, she pulled herself out of her mind. The memories felt warped, but they also felt real. Maybe she really had killed someone—it was the only explanation she could think of.

The corners of her mouth ticked down in frustration, and she aimed a vicious kick at the air in front of her.

Ruby imagined weapons in her hands, from gleaming daggers to heavy clubs, carefully gauging how the weapons would affect her movement in combat.

She carefully wiped away the thin sheen of sweat over her brow, and she noted the slight tremors of anticipation in her hands. Bloodlust had made her jittery, she wanted to taste victory today.

Familiar footsteps echoed down the stairs. She sat down on her cot and pasted a bored expression on her face.

The nobleman's henchmen opened Ruby's door and gathered all of her empty bowls. This was her freedom, in some twisted way, and she could do little else but glare from her cot.

"It's time," the man said dramatically. He held the door open, even though it stayed open on its own. "Your first challenge awaits you."

"What happens if I run?" Ruby asked curiously. She wasn't actually planning on bolting—she just wanted to find a weakness in his annoyingly pleasant armor. "What would your king do to you?"

His hands shot out, and something cold clasped around Ruby's wrists before she could react. "It's fortunate we don't have to worry about that, isn't it?" the man said, as though he'd just won something.

"Shackling my hands doesn't mean I can't run," Ruby darted forward, and when she turned back, there was genuine panic in the man's eyes.

"You imbeciles!" the man roared at the two men that were trying to carry all of Ruby's bowls. "What would you have done if she escaped? Nothing! I should have you two battle to the death, and she'll kill the winner!"

Ruby almost felt sorry for them. She was surprised that

the man could get so angry—he'd always seemed rather calm to her. After he had finished berating his men, he turned to Ruby.

"As for you," he said in a controlled voice, "you are underground in a kingdom that wants you dead. I assure you that you wouldn't get very far."

"How did you put it?" Ruby fought the urge to mockingly tap her chin. "Ah, yes. You said that I could ruin this kingdom."

"Well, that's only if no one wants you dead. Unfortunately for you, if you did manage to escape, anyone is allowed to kill you. Trust me—they would tear you apart in a second, with or without a reward."

The man was too free with this information. Ruby had long suspected that lie after lie fell from his lips. Still, there was nothing to be done. The nobleman placed an insistent hand on the middle of her back and pushed her up the stairs in front of him.

Ruby heard the metallic clang of the door being locked behind them.

After a few minutes of walking through a labyrinth of corridors, they emerged in a dusty corridor. Paint chipped off the walls, and cobwebs blanketed the ground. It looked as if no one had been there in years.

"Someone needs to take better care of this place," the man said, clicking his tongue. "After all, it's where the greatest events in the kingdom take place."

Before Ruby could ask what those events were, she heard the distant roar of cheers. They rumbled through the hallway and almost shook the building. Instead of following the raucous shouting, the man shoved her into a side room she hadn't noticed.

One of the henchmen locked the door behind them before undoing Ruby's shackles. She looked around and realized she was in a small room that held a huge array of weapons.

"Now, would you prefer a spear or a hammer?" the man asked Ruby.

"Which one would you rather die by? I'll choose the opposite."

He laughed. "You're a funny girl. You can kill me, if you want. Go ahead."

The man spread his arms, as if inviting her to try.

"And what if I do?" she asked after pulling a hammer down from one of the shelves.

"Well, my men would take you down, of course. Look at them!"

She did, and she saw the distinct glint of metal protruding from their belts. They both smiled at her as though they would enjoy killing her with one of the various weapons they wore.

"What if I think it's worth it?" she asked mildly, taking a threatening step toward the nobleman.

"You are, of course, free to think whatever you would like," the man said. "There isn't much left in this world that I haven't seen. Death wouldn't be unwelcome. Dare I say, though, that I think you would very much mind dying, since all you've seen—oh, forgive me, all you *remember* seeing—is a prison cell. Do you really want to die with no more than that as your legacy? Such a shame."

"I've known, for some time now, that you are the reason I can't remember anything." Ruby said quietly, seething with anger.

He slowly backed away from her. "Well, yes, it's true. I was the one who knocked you unconscious."

Ruby's rage-filled eyes blazed into his, and she turned on her heel, stalking toward the racks of weapons. She didn't want to admit it, but the man was right. She didn't want to die only remembering the four walls of a prison cell. She wanted to understand who she was, and then, she wanted to get away from this kingdom.

She hefted an ornate hammer and frowned. Its weight felt wrong in her hand. Ruby set it back down and felt her gaze drawn to an intricately carved spear. It called to her, its presence somehow familiar in the sea of unknown.

Ruby took her time looking through the weapons. She wanted the time to strategize for the battle ahead. The orc was going to be a large foe, even though they were supposedly only a half-orc. A half-orc would still be fairly large and would most likely rely on brute strength over cunning. She needed a plan.

Ruby was small, and if her agility was truly as impressive as the man claimed, she would be quick and evasive. If she wanted to go down that route, she would need a light, nimble weapon to keep up with her quick attacks.

She brought the spear down from the shelf and turned to face the three men. "I've chosen."

"Excellent!" the noble reached over the rack and produced a round, similarly carved shield. "For that spear, you get a complimentary shield. Maybe you will survive, after all."

"What's the orc going to use?" Ruby asked, accepting the shield from the man.

"Half-orc."

"What's the half-orc going to use?" Ruby didn't bother giving him a reaction.

"You're about to find out." the man smiled mysteriously.

They waited in silence.

"What happens now?" Ruby asked, and the man simply waved at her.

Suddenly, Ruby was falling. She stifled a surprised scream and clutched her weapons tightly as she fell into the arena.

"Stupid girl," a guard said once she'd fallen. He let go of the chain he'd pulled to open the trapdoor.

The crowd in the stands laughed raucously, and Ruby felt a surge of white-hot anger. She tamped it down, knowing that she would need her wits about her if she were to best a half-orc.

She quickly scanned the arena. There were bales of hay on one side, strategically placed to serve as temporary hiding spots, and large boulders sat on the other side. That was unfortunate—she wasn't nearly strong enough to move the boulders, but she guessed that the half-orc would be.

The crowd went wild, and Ruby's eyes widened as the half-orc stomped into the arena. She'd been right about his size—he was monstrous, at least three times as big as she was, and he was armed with a huge, double-bladed axe.

The half-orc's face was just as gruesome. Its mouth was open in a roar, his ugly, yellow teeth came to sharp points, and spittle flew out of his mouth when he bellowed at her again. His obsidian eyes burned with murderous rage.

The announcer was shouting enthusiastically. Ruby strained to hear him over the cheers, and she managed to make out the last of his words.

"With the previous bout over, and what a bloody rally it was, the next is about to begin! Two murderers are going to face off in our toughest battle yet! Get your bets in now! Who will it be—the girl, or the orc?"

"Half-orc!"

Even over the roars of the audience, Ruby recognized the nobleman's voice and barely suppressed the urge to roll her eyes.

She saw a flash of purple out of the corner of her eye, but it wasn't him. It was a glass box full of other nobles who looked just like him.

Ruby scoffed at the idea that they thought a flimsy barrier

like that would be able to stop her. In her gut she knew that she wasn't the killer they had taken her to be, but she had the sinking suspicion that she'd been trained to fight. Before she could reflect any further, the half-orc charged.

The half-orc wore a black mask over the bottom half of his face, and the white skull in the center of it sent a chill skittering up her spine. He was fast. Within moments, the half-orc was upon her, and he raised his axe above his head before swinging it through the air.

Ruby leapt out of the way, rolling to dodge the powerful blow, and the beast roared, hefting his weapon and slamming it down into the ground, barely missing his agile foe. The sharpened blade of his axe glinted as the half-orc wrenched it out of the dirt, and he turned once more, seething hatred in his eyes.

"I will crush you," he growled, and the half-orc swung again, barely missing Ruby's head.

She seized the moment and launched herself up the axe's wooden shaft, quickly dashing up his arm and sinking her spear into the bulging muscles in his shoulder. The half-orc's meaty hand batted uselessly at his deep wound, and he groaned as blood seeped through his fingers.

"What's wrong? Did you hurt yourself?" Ruby goaded him, she needed him to be blind with anger. "Do you need a giant bandage for your giant, clumsy self?"

Another roar, another attack. The half-orc lost himself to rage as he swung at her blindly.

Ruby stepped back and lost her balance on a loose stone. Fighting to regain her balance, she cursed when a line of searing pain shot up her arm. She covered the new wound with her other hand and clutched it for a moment as warm blood splattered on the dirt below.

Everything was red, but the fight wasn't over.

The half-orc smiled victoriously. It was as if he had real-

17

ized for the first time that Ruby couldn't avoid him forever, and this newfound confidence spurred him through another series of attacks.

He struck again, and Ruby rolled forward, scrabbling away from his wild swings. It was impossible to ignore the pain in her arm, and her senses were starting to dull from the blood loss. If she didn't win soon, she wasn't going to win at all.

Ruby had to think. As she dodged the constant attacks and grew closer and closer to losing consciousness, she realized he was getting angrier. He was falling back into his blind rage, and though it was difficult to think through the pain, it was still far from impossible.

Ruby ran behind one of the boulders. The half-orc immediately sent it rolling towards her, as though he'd been waiting for a chance to make use of the giant rocks. Each time, she made sure to barely dodge out of the way, and with each push on the boulders, the half-orc grew slower and weaker.

On the last one, it looked as if it took almost all of his strength to push it towards her. Moving carefully, Ruby ducked behind the boulder like she had every other time. When he pushed on it, she ran at the wall instead of away. She jumped at the wall and pushed off it, landing in front of the boulder as it crashed into the wall.

As expected, the half-orc's momentum sent him stumbling towards her, and he broke his fall with his palms. Ruby snarled and seized the opportunity, letting loose a scream that held every emotion within her. She pierced him through the back of the neck with her spear, and blood spurted out of his fatal wound.

His big hands groped uselessly over his wound, and a crimson pool of his blood stained the ground red.

"You're not very bright, are you?" Ruby asked.

Panic and rage combined to create something far deadlier than either of those emotions alone. The half-orc swiped at her again, and she plunged her spear into his eye. Ruby grimaced at the spray of blood and tried to hold on as the half-orc collapsed in a cloud of dust.

His lifeless hand fell away from the ruined remains of his eye, and Ruby tried to ignore the terrible squelch as she pulled her spear out of the socket.

It was done. She had won.

Ruby raised both of her arms in victory, and the crowd's thunderous applause shook the ground she stood on.

As Ruby turned to acknowledge the spectators, she saw two guards beckoning her over to the trapdoor she had fallen from. Her adrenaline began to wane, and the pain of her arm came back to her. She looked down at her wound, noticing that in the heat of battle, she hadn't seen how deep it actually was.

She stumbled toward one of the guards, who caught her around her waist.

"She needs a nurse!" another guard yelled through the trapdoor. Ruby faded in and out of consciousness, but she noticed the ladder that sat against the back of the wall.

Somehow, they hauled her up the ladder, and her head lolled against one of the guard's shoulders. When they reached the top, the noble's henchman took her weapons from her. She would have laughed, but she was too weak. She was in no state to bring harm to anyone.

It was only when she realized that she was being taken back to her prison cell that panic started to set in.

THE MAN'S BEARD

distant pulling sensation roused her from her deep slumber, and Ruby jolted awake before sagging in a mixture of exhaustion and relief when she looked around her prison cell. A woman in a simple dress slowly reached out, and she continued to carefully wrap the bandage around her arm.

A feeling of familiarity kicked in when she looked around at the prison walls and felt the hard cot under her back. The woman tending to her wound finished and looked down at Ruby's face. There was no fear in her eyes, and Ruby wondered why she had assumed there might have been.

"The bleeding took a very long time to stop…any longer, and you would probably be dead," she said.

"Oh." Ruby found herself at a loss for words.

The woman stopped for a moment to lift a small bowl up to Ruby's lips. "Drink this. You'll need all of your energy to get through your recovery period."

Clear water glistened in the bowl. Ruby took it gratefully and drained the bowl in seconds before asking for more, to which the woman laughed.

"Don't overdo yourself," she smiled kindly, though she took the empty bowl and handed it to the noble's henchmen that stood outside of the door. "Tell Woodruff that she's awake, and fetch more water, at least two or three bowls," the woman instructed the burly guards.

One of them nodded and hurried away. The woman returned to Ruby's side and inspected her work, seemingly pleased with the result.

"There isn't much more I can do for it," she informed Ruby.

Ruby grimaced as she shifted her arm.

"You'll just have to be strong enough to fight off infection and survive more possible blood loss. You shouldn't move for the next few days. When you feel as if you can, tell one of the guards, and Woodruff will come for you."

"That's his name?" Ruby couldn't help but smile a little at that. "It's quite silly."

"Do not disrespect the nobles," the woman snapped. She glanced back toward the henchman that remained.

"Why not?" Ruby asked, tilting her head. She said it quietly, but the woman seemed too scared to explain, and Ruby wanted her to know that whatever she was hiding, she could trust Ruby with her secret.

"Just don't." The woman stood abruptly and dusted off her dress. "They will bring you water. It may take some time for you to be able to eat after such a terrible injury, so I have already told them to wait until tonight. If you don't feel like you can eat, you do not have to."

"Wait!" Ruby tried to sit up. "Please."

"I must go." The woman practically raced out of the cell when the remaining henchman opened the door for her.

"Who are you?" Ruby asked, switching targets and trying to appeal to the guard.

He eyed her and then turned away.

She cleared her throat. "I asked you a question."

Still, the henchman said nothing. She reached an arm through the gate and gripped the back of his shirt. Yanking him back against the metal bars, she asked him again. "Who are you?"

He turned and ripped himself out of her grasp, seizing her wrist before she could pull it back through. He twisted it painfully—it was the same arm with her wound.

"Mind yourself," he growled before letting her go and facing the hallway once more.

Soon after, the second henchman returned. Ruby had gone back to her cot, but at the sight of water, she approached the metal bars once more.

"Not so fast," the henchman Ruby had spoken to said. He took the bowl of water from the other man with a malicious glint in his eye.

"Give it to me!" Ruby reached through the bars and tried to snatch it, ignoring the throbbing ache from her wound. "Woodruff's orders!"

"She's right," the other henchman remarked. Ruby noticed the scruffy beard on his face—for some reason, that suddenly stuck out to her, as though it had triggered a memory of something in her past. Perhaps her father, whoever he was, had a beard like that. She had a faint vision of a crooning melody being sung to her as she was rocked back and forth, the memory of the scratchy beard sticking with her. But nothing further came to her.

"She'll get her water eventually, once she apologizes." The clean-shaven guard turned to face her after he had spoken.

"You don't deserve it! You're keeping me captive."

"Then maybe you don't deserve all of your water." The man gestured carelessly with the bowl, and water sloshed over the sides.

Ruby glared at him and crossed her arms defiantly. "I'll tell Woodruff."

"If he cared about you, you wouldn't be in a prison cell right now," the henchman's lips twisted into a smirk, and he tipped the bowl again.

"Fine!" Ruby said. "Stop. I'm sorry."

"For?"

"For reaching through the bar and grabbing the back of your shirt. I didn't know a big man like you could get so offended by a little girl like me." Ruby glared at him menacingly. "Now, give me my water!"

In a fit of anger, the man tossed it on the floor at her feet. It landed upright, but there was hardly any water remaining.

"Take it, prisoner."

The man turned around again, but not before Ruby caught the glint of satisfaction in his eyes. But what truly surprised her was the expression on the other guard's face.

Sorry, he mouthed at her, and there was a genuine apology in his eyes before he turned.

Ruby drank up the last few drops of water left in the bowl and spent the rest of the day begging for more. She hated how pathetic she sounded, but just as she had planned, she eventually got through to the bearded henchman.

"Where are you going?" the second one demanded as the sympathetic guard started to walk away.

"I'm going to get her water."

"Get back here!"

"Woodruff's orders were to get her as much water as she needs. That's what I'm doing. You aren't in charge of me."

"She doesn't deserve it!"

Without another word, the bearded man walked up the stairs. He returned moments later with a bowl of water, full to the brim, and Ruby looked at it longingly. Before his angry partner could ruin anything, the bearded one slid the water through the bars, and Ruby took it gratefully. She retreated back to her cot and drank all of it, feeling much more refreshed.

"Thank you," she said genuinely. The man with the beard dipped his head and smiled.

The other one shoved him and hissed something into his ear before returning to his post. The bearded one smiled at Ruby before turning back around.

Later on in the day, Woodruff paid her a visit.

"Would you listen to me if I told you that one of your henchmen is insufferable?" Ruby asked him.

"Oh, really?" Woodruff asked before glancing at his men. "Which would that be?"

"The one without the beard. He refused me water."

"Oh, you poor girl." Woodruff wagged a finger at the culprit and scolded him with a smile on his face. "Don't abuse her again!"

He turned back to Ruby. "Is that what you wanted?"

"As soon as I'm free, I'm killing him."

"Well, you'd end up right back here, having to face another murderer in the arena, won't you? What a sight that would be."

Ruby crossed her arms. "What do you want, Woodruff?"

"You know my name? That's a development." He stroked his beard with his fingers. "I only came to tell you that you fought well, and your first challenge is officially complete!" He paused as though he expected fireworks to go off, and then he continued. "Your second one awaits. How is your arm?"

"Fine." Ruby moved it around, doing her best not to flinch at the pain. She didn't care about what the nurse said—she wanted to complete these challenges and be free as soon as she could.

"That's not what your nurse told me, but I like your spirit!" Woodruff smiled. "Has your memory returned at all? Tell me everything."

"Nothing's come back to me. It's all blank." Woodruff nodded like he wanted Ruby to say more, but she didn't know what else to tell him. She didn't even know if she trusted him, but she tried. "I don't know where I've come from. I don't remember my parent's names, if I had siblings, I don't even know what I'm doing in this kingdom, since you said it's not my home. I don't remember anything." Ruby chose to leave out that some things she saw, like the guard's beard, seemed to trigger something in her memory.

Woodruff took a moment to respond and made a great show of mulling over her words. "Very strange, that is. I'm starting to think this is perhaps a little deeper than a simple concussion—perhaps your own mind is blocking out the memories? That is a defense mechanism, you know, much more common than you'd think. When a person does something horrible, their mind makes them forget, so they are able to go on surviving rather than trying to find a way to live with themselves after what they've done."

"I'm not…" Ruby hesitated.

She wanted to tell Woodruff she didn't do it, that deep down, she knew she couldn't be capable of that, but she didn't say a word.

"Not what?"

"Forget it."

"Don't you worry. I will do some research on this phenomenon to see if I can find anything that would help you unblock your memory. It may require magic and take some time. Show your loyalty and respect for the law and I'm sure we can solve this problem." His lips spread into a thin smile.

"Yes." Ruby grimaced, she had responded too eagerly. Then, she realized what Woodruff had said—magic. Was that his own way of subconsciously confirming that her memory had not, in fact, disappeared on its own?

"Very well. In the meantime, it is time you learn of your next task."

"What is it?" Ruby asked.

"You must bring the kingdom five dragon scales. Where and how is up to you, and I do hope you survive, but don't worry—it's okay if you don't. This task is a difficult one, probably more so than defeating a half-orc, so don't be too goal-oriented."

Ruby shook her head in disbelief at how strange Woodruff sounded. "Why does your kingdom want dragon scales?"

"They have a very specific use, one which we cannot share with you."

"Oh, I see. You think you can send me to my death and not give me a reason for it?"

"I did give you a reason...you have to retrieve the dragon scales."

"But I want to know why you need them. Is that so wrong?"

"Yes." Woodruff didn't even hesitate. "Yes, it is. Now, if you would like help, such as where to even find a dragon, I would love to tell you, but you do have to do one thing for me."

"What?"

"Stop nagging." Woodruff waited, expecting Ruby to start another argument, and even though she crossed her arms angrily, she stayed quiet.

Satisfied, he continued. "We've received reports of a dragon being spotted by a nearby mountain. It shouldn't be too hard to find its cave once you're up there, and then, you simply must take the scales. To both assist and monitor you on your quest, we are giving you a squire. If you flee, you will die immediately. If your squire does not return, you will die immediately. If you are successful, you will…" Woodruff drummed his fingers on his leg. "Not die immediately! You will be free to go, but you will never be allowed back into our kingdom again."

"How would you even kill me if I flee?" Ruby asked, tired of Woodruff's dramatic airs. Squires are weak—definitely not as strong as an orc."

"Half-orc!"

"Whatever!" Ruby resisted the urge to slam her fist into the wall.

"Do you want your questions answered or not?" Woodruff asked. "I could send you out there blindly and let you find out for yourself what happens if you flee. How does that sound?"

"Fine! Just tell me!"

"Will you behave?"

"Yes."

"Sometimes, I feel as if you forget that you are, in fact, our prisoner. If I wasn't warming up to you, I would be much harsher on you right now. We are being far kinder to you than you deserve after killing someone. You understand that, don't you?"

"Yes," Ruby acquiesced softly. "Please, just tell me what would happen if I ran."

Woodruff raised his eyebrows. "You're still planning on fleeing?"

"It's what prisoners do, isn't it?"

Woodruff laughed. "Fair enough."

He motioned toward the beardless henchman, who disappeared up the stairs.

While he was gone, Woodruff spoke. "I wouldn't be surprised if you had decided to run off, which is why we have a special gift, just for you!" He waited until his henchman returned, carrying a silver headdress with the wings of a dragon on either side. "Put this on."

Ruby took the gaudy piece, surprised that it even fit through the bars, and held it in her hands to examine it. It glimmered in the low light, and though it had not been made of real dragon bone, it was just as elegant.

"What if I don't?" Ruby asked.

"I'll make it smaller and force it onto that big head of yours so that you're in constant pain."

Ruby put it on.

"Good!" Woodruff exclaimed, clapping his hands. "Now, try to take it off."

Ruby tried. She pulled at it, and it was stuck firmly in position. "What kind of trick is this?"

"That headdress is now bound to you, and you are unable to remove it."

"You cursed it?" The first feelings of anxiety rose in Ruby's stomach—she couldn't remember anything about curses, but something told her that it was dangerous to mess with that kind of magic.

"No, of course not. It is very similar in nature to a cursed object, but it's not cursed. It's more like a deadline. It belongs to a certain friend of mine, and when it is out of her possession, the wearer has a week to return it before the headdress kills them. Through its special connection to her, it also has a connection to this kingdom. Therefore, if you harm anyone wearing the king's seal, the headdress will kill you. Only if you return with the five dragon scales will you be granted your freedom. Understand?"

"Yes," Ruby breathed. This mission was a heavy one, and it very well could kill her. When she found out that she was going to fight the half-orc, she hadn't had time to worry. She was thrown into the arena immediately and had to focus on surviving. Now, with another perilous mission looming over her head, she could do nothing but worry.

Woodruff's henchmen came down the stairs with giant boxes, and Ruby was shocked to realize that she hadn't even noticed they'd left.

Woodruff beckoned them over.

"Now, these won't be able to fit through the bars," Woodruff said. They opened the boxes and pulled out a battle-worn suit of armor, a spear, and a shield, all of which bore the crest of the kingdom. Elegant dragon scales were engraved on everything to match the headdress she wore. "Your squire will be here shortly to help you into the armor. This is kingdom property, and we wish you success on your journey, but if you perish, we would very much appreciate it if you died somewhere that would make it easy for the squire to return your equipment."

"Seriously?" Ruby asked, her eyebrows raised. The noble's comment served to do nothing but annoy her.

"Yes, seriously!" Woodruff looked offended. "All of this is very expensive—you don't understand just how much of a fortune these things cost! If your body doesn't return, we want the equipment—your squire knows this as well."

"I'll do my best, sir." Ruby dropped into a mocking curtsy. The bearded henchman smiled, but the other henchman and Woodruff didn't.

"You had better, or we'll leave your body to the vultures instead of at least cremating you as a criminal. Now, I must go. I have many responsibilities to take care of. Good luck."

Woodruff left, his henchmen following behind him. The gleaming armor from the open boxes taunted her from the other side of the prison's metal bars.

THE GOOD ONES

*R*uby paced back and forth in her cramped cell.

She'd never slain a dragon before—that much she could feel deep down in her bones, though she did know she'd been raised to fight. Perhaps that was why Woodruff believed she could complete this quest, though he had made it abundantly clear that he thought she wouldn't survive it.

Footsteps sounded down the stairs. A very handsome, scruffy man with a brown beard the same color as his wavy hair entered the room with a curious smile on his face. He looked as if he was only a few years older than Ruby, and she stood as he approached.

"We lead very different lives, don't we?" Ruby asked absent-mindedly. "I'm young and imprisoned for murder. You're young and on the other side of the bars."

"Yet here we are, both about to embark on a quest with a very high risk of dying," the man sighed.

Ruby shrugged, and he went on to his next question. "I'm going to go out on a limb and ask you to kindly not murder me. Can you make that promise?"

"Fine." She paused. "I don't know how you do things in Torbek, but you're a little old for a squire."

"Yes, yes, most squires are children, I know," the squire laughed. "Though I can't imagine even a kingdom such as this one would send a child to fight dragons or guard you on the way. A babysitter is usually older than the baby they are sitting, are they not?"

Ruby rolled her eyes. "Very well, you've made your point."

Still, the man continued with his explanation. "I am not of noble blood, so I cannot obtain knighthood as easily as some others. As such, I must first complete an extraordinary task before I can be knighted. In this case, that is escorting you so that you may return with the five dragon scales." The man's eyes shone. "Then, I will be a knight. All you have to do is to not run away."

"This quest doesn't seem all that extraordinary, if you ask me," Ruby eyed the squire.

"Your comment has been disregarded because I did not ask you," the man scoffed. "Besides, I'm willing to bet that you've never stared a dragon in the eyes. It's enough to cause even the strongest warriors of all time to flinch. If that's not any indication of what fearsome creatures dragons are, just take a look at the armor." Ruby did, and she suddenly noticed the dents in it. "What do you think those marks are, hmm? Marks from having to drag the armor home after the last… misadventure, mixed in with some claw marks, you think? I'm sure Woodruff has told you what I'm really here to keep an eye on."

"He said to die conveniently so that you can recover the armor." Ruby's eyes twinkled. "Maybe, just for fun, I'll die very inconveniently. Then, you'll never be a knight."

It was the man's turn to roll his eyes. "It had better not come to that, but just in case it does, I've been trained for this."

"Oh, really?" Ruby leaned forward, entertaining him. "What kind of impossible training does a brave squire have to go through to be ready for an inconvenient death?"

"We train to be prepared," the squire gave her a conspiratorial wink. "Now, have you worn armor before?"

"I'm not sure, sir squire. I don't have any of my memories of before I woke up down here, locked away until I could face my doom. In this case, the doom is you."

"My name is Dirk!" he said, and Ruby had to cover her mouth to stifle her laughter. "As for your memory loss," he added with a shrug, "unfortunately, it happens. Now, what do you know about your ability to fight?"

"Well, Dirk," Ruby said, tapping her finger on her chin, "I just killed a half-orc, which, dare I say, I'm rather proud of."

"Oh, I'm sure you are. Foolish little adventurers, always believing themselves capable of anything after just one battle."

"Sounds kind of like knights, if you ask me."

"Once again, I didn't!"

"Yeah, yeah, just show me how to put the armor on, squire."

"Very well." Dirk pulled a key out and unlocked Ruby's door. He guided her through the steps. "Undershirt first, then the leather, then put the metal armor on like a jacket. You clasp it in the front underneath the metal, like this." Dirk demonstrated, though Ruby couldn't help but laugh at him as he struggled. He shot her a glare but ignored her. "Now, the pants. Leggings, then the metal wraps around them."

"What, no leather?" Ruby asked.

"No. You are very unlikely to be attacked below the belt. The leather around your chest is to soften any blow you may take from the dragon, and you had better hope it does, or you're dead."

"Seems dumb to me." Ruby could tell that with every jab

at Dirk, he was getting more and more fed up with her. "Whatever, I'll do it," Ruby said, to keep him from going crazy. "Hand it over." He took all of it off and dropped it at her feet. "Well, aren't you rude."

"Hey," Dirk said, raising his hands in the air as though he was innocent, "I've treated you just as you've treated me—nothing more, nothing less." He smirked and left Ruby in her cell to change.

The leather was tight around her chest, but she put it on anyways. She felt strange in the armor, however. It was tight in some places, loose in others, and all in all, the armor made it incredibly difficult to move. She did admire the designs, which went nicely with her headdress. The intricate, curling dragons were carved all over the metal. She could almost understand not wanting to lose such a beautiful piece of protection. Almost.

Dirk returned a while later, and Ruby just sat there in her armor until he did.

"I have a genuine question," she started, tapping her foot impatiently, "what made you think it would possibly take me all that time to change? I was ready not even ten minutes after you left."

"Forgive me for wanting to give you some privacy. Besides, why are you in such a rush to die?" Dirk inspected Ruby's armor and pulled the latches apart with a sigh. "No, you've done it all wrong! You forgot these straps on the sides, and you've clasped the wrong parts together over here. You truly are a mess, aren't you?"

Ruby felt his warm hands tugging at the various straps. She felt awkward while he did and refused to meet his eyes, but she let him help her.

"Excellent," he said when he was finished, "it fits you quite well. Can you walk better?"

Ruby took a few steps around her cell. It still felt strange and unnecessary, but she knew she would be thankful for it when she faced a dragon and didn't burn to ash.

She gave him a reluctant nod.

"Perfect! Now, your training. Come along with me." Dirk opened the cell door, regarding Ruby with a wary expression. She stepped outside her cell door, hesitating for a moment, and then trailed after the squire as he strode through the dim corridors.

"Where are you taking me?"

"This corridor should do. It's very much like a dragon's den." Dirk pulled a sword from a sheath Ruby hadn't noticed. She was taken by surprise when he lunged at her, and she tripped over a few loose tiles as she dodged his quick jab.

"What are you doing?" Ruby asked, but Dirk ignored her.

"Come on, now, you must be more agile than that! Otherwise, this will be a very short adventure, and a full belly for the dragon." Dirk kept swiping at her.

Ruby knew how to dodge swords, but the armor made it extremely difficult.

She managed to roll towards him when dodging one of his blows, shouldering him out of the way to get to her spear. She grabbed it and turned to face Dirk as he got up.

"Clever," he said, "but that would likely not work on a dragon—it would simply step on you, and maybe add some fire for the fun of it."

"You're wrong." Ruby lunged at Dirk, and he batted her spear away with his sword. Ruby had to remember that her weapon was weaker than a sword in terms of them clashing, and it was made more for throwing than for jabbing. It was just barely longer than Dirk's sword. She realized that she would have to get up close to the dragon when she fought it.

"How so?" Dirk asked. He swung for Ruby's head, and she ducked. He was getting serious about this, and Ruby would have worried that he truly was trying to kill her if she wasn't dressed completely in armor.

"Well, dragons are big." Ruby dodged another swing and saw a pattern to Dirk's attacks—he always aimed high, then low. Ruby caught on and found her own pattern, ending it with a twist and pressing her spear to his chest. "Big things are always clumsier than little things. Yes, the dragon could step on me, but not if I get out of the way in time. I'm quicker than the dragon, and I could trip it up by getting in between its feet and stabbing it until it's so angry that it isn't even thinking anymore. It'll be careless, blowing fire all over the place, and I'll have a chance to land a strike that will end in the dragon's death."

"You're smart when you talk about the dragon," Dirk said with a smirk, "but not when you're fighting with me." He kicked one of his feet out at Ruby's knee, not hard enough to do any damage, but hard enough that Ruby felt the pain for a moment. Dirk twisted to the side, and it was faster than Ruby could recover. Moments later, he had her spear pinned to the wall and the tip of his sword at her throat.

"Fine, you win." Ruby rolled her eyes.

Dirk didn't let her go. "Yes, the armor does seem to fit you well."

Ruby scoffed and pushed him out of the way, carelessly letting his sword scrape against her armor. "Careful, or it'll be damaged before we even leave."

"You wouldn't!" Dirk said, his voice high pitched and full of offense. He cleared his throat and spoke again in his normal, deeper voice. "You wouldn't." He shook his head when he saw Ruby watching him, laughter on the edge of her lips. "Just remember how much trouble you'll be in if that armor gets too damaged."

"In that case I think I'd be dead," Ruby scoffed. "So I wouldn't worry about the armor."

"Ah! You admit it!" Dirk pointed at Ruby. "You might die."

"I said *if*."

"You aren't as sure as yourself as you'd like me to think, are you, prisoner?" Dirk laughed. "I've met your kind before," he said, hesitating for a moment, then glancing away. "Be careful—your confidence just might be your death, and I think you're starting to realize it." He tapped his cheek as though he was deep in thought. "I'll be back for you in an hour—we'll head out and camp at the foothills for the night. Oh!" Dirk returned to her cell and grabbed her spear. "Almost forgot this."

"But that's mine now!" Ruby said, going to the bars of her cell. "You really don't trust me with my weapon when you've just bested me? What could I possibly do with it? It's not like these bars can be broken. And it's not as if I can leave and not die." Ruby pointed at her headdress.

"Stop worrying! It's just protocol. You'll have your spear again soon." Dirk shook his head as he locked Ruby's cell up behind her. "Always in a rush to die," he murmured to himself before leaving.

While Ruby waited for his return, she thought about everything he had said, about how he had analyzed her. He was right, of course, Ruby did need to put on a tough act, but did he truly not understand why?

Ruby paced around her room and began talking to the other prisoners, who had been silent almost every time Ruby had a visitor. "Does he not get it? I need to act tough! I mean, I wake up with no memories, I have no idea who I am, and I'm suddenly expected to fight an orc?"

"Half-orc," one of the other prisoners corrected, and the others laughed.

Ruby ignored it. "He throws me into that first mission, of course I'm worried about dying! And now, I have to face a dragon that no one's apparently faced and lived before?"

Ruby paused and shook her head. "If I don't act tough, then I won't think I'm tough. If I don't believe in myself, then it really is a suicide mission." She shook her head. "As long as I stay optimistic, I'll survive. As long as I believe I can get through this, I'll survive."

"You sound just like Mara," one of the prisoners remarked. Ruby hadn't heard his voice before.

"Mara?"

"She, too, was faced with your quests after murdering the king's son."

"She did that?" Ruby asked, but she knew the answer—not because the man who was speaking said she had, but because that familiar tingling feeling had taken root in her head. She'd heard of this before she forgot who she was. She was sure of it.

"Yes. She told us her whole story, that Mara. Said the king's son insulted her family and said some horrible things to her when she was out in the market. They'd met before—I'd seen it myself—and many of us assumed they were seeing each other, but that day was a horrible one. I don't know what else the king's son had done to her, but it must have been horrible. It was enough for her to kill him, right there in the middle of the square, and as soon as she had, she fell to her knees and wept. She was thrown down here. She faced an orc, I believe, not a half-orc, and she only barely managed to win. She returned to the dungeon in critical condition. A nurse never left her side, and all the while, the rest of us heard her optimism. 'I can get through this,' she would say. 'I'm strong. I'll recover. I'll survive—it's what I've always done.'"

"Did she?" Ruby asked, even though the answer was obvious. For a while, the man was quiet, and Ruby didn't think he would answer.

"No," he said solemnly. There was a heavy silence in the

air. "She left to face the dragon, even as her insides were falling out, and she never returned. I think it was what the king intended, for her to die without him directly causing it. He likes to be known as a merciful king, so he sent Mara on a mission he knew she would not come back from, and the most heartbreaking thing of it all was that she truly believed she would win. It was the last thing she said before she left. She told us she would slay the dragon and be back." The man paused. "That kid's right, you know—that squire of yours. Confidence can very well get you killed."

"How am I supposed to think of this mission, then? Act hopeless? As if I won't survive? If I do that, no matter what happens, it'll be true."

"Do what you will, girl. Believe what you must, but don't let it kill you. That's often how death gets the good ones."

"Thank you," Ruby said, and the dungeon was silent once more.

DRAGONS, DWARVES, AND DIRK

*A*n hour later, Dirk had returned.

After hearing Mara's story, Ruby sat on her cot, deep in thought. Somehow, she knew that she was strong enough to slay the dragon, but what if it was just foolish thinking? What if her belief in herself would really get her killed?

Ruby also tried to remember who she was. The harder she fought against her mental barriers, the more her memories were blocked off, and she knew that if she killed the dragon, that would be her best chance to recover her memories. The thought of getting answers was the only thing that kept her going.

Even though he had forced Ruby to fight a half-orc, she trusted Woodruff to find a solution. He'd made her a promise that she intended to hold him to when she returned and was set free of her cell. If he tricked her, she might have just to fall apart, but she hoped he wouldn't do that. It was all that she could hold on to.

"Ah, you look even more afraid than before," Dirk said when he returned, a teasing smile on his lips. "I've brought you food to eat on the way. Come," he said, once her cell was unlocked, "the wagon is waiting."

"How far away is the dragon?" Ruby asked as Dirk guided her up the steps once more. They left through a side door, and she gasped in wonder.

"It's not about the distance—it's about the creatures we'll meet on the way." Dirk watched Ruby's expression with interest written all over his face. "Fascinating, isn't it? Palaces truly are a beautiful sight."

They'd emerged from the hallway out into a sinking sun. The evening air was cool around them, and shadows darkened the empty streets, but that didn't make the palace look any less elegant.

It seemed to be made entirely of glass and shimmering blue metal. Spires dazzled in the last rays of sunlight, and there were too many of them to even count. Designs in a peculiar repeating pattern took her attention. The image was repeated on a few flags that waved idly in the gentle breeze.

"The Torbek family banner," Dirk explained, noticing her interest. "Through there," he added, striding toward a door covered with intricate glass decorations. A few servants paused in their labors, glancing over suspiciously as they exited. Ruby finally emerged outside and took a deep breath to take in the rich smell of nature.

After a moment,

Ruby turned away from the stunning palace and found an old, rickety wagon with a torn covering and an ancient looking horse.

"This is what we're taking?" she asked, remembering how the other prisoner had said that the purpose of Mara's quest was for it to kill her. Ruby could already see it. Their wagon would fall apart, or the old horse would die, and the two of them would have to walk the remaining distance, it all seemed too likely. The reality of the quest set in, and Ruby was terrified.

Dirk got into the wagon first, and Ruby followed.

"It should be around two days of travel," he said, taking the reins and spurring the horse on its way. The horse seemed to walk slower than Ruby did. "Maybe three," he sighed.

"I'm not surprised that they give us the worst possible transportation they could have," Ruby commented. She grabbed her spear from where it lay on top of a sack of food and a few canteens of water.

"If I may ask, why are you in such a rush to die?"

"I'm not!"

"Yes, you are."

She grimaced. "I don't know, I just want this whole thing to be over. I want to know who I am." Ruby paused. "You don't know what it's like to wake up in a dungeon cell with next to no memories of yourself, just to be told that you'd killed someone and that to be redeemed, you have to kill a very angry half-orc, then steal a dragon's scales."

"I bet I can guess," Dirk said quietly. "Horrible, right?"

Ruby nodded. "Horrible."

"I truly am sorry that you have to go through this," Dirk said, and it was the most genuine thing Ruby had ever heard him say.

"Aw, Dirky!" Ruby exclaimed with false cheer, smirking as she clasped her hands in front of her heart.

Dirk's face reddened, and he glared at her. "Stop that."

"Why? I thought we were having a moment." Ruby pouted at him to keep herself from chuckling, but he was suddenly very focused on the old horse.

"We were! Can't you let anything be genuine?" Dirk looked away. Ruby could tell he meant the question, even though there was a light tone of voice behind it, and it was her turn to be embarrassed.

"Well, I don't have much experience with genuine moments, you know, with the whole memory loss thing," Ruby tried to explain.

"Doesn't mean you have to be so sarcastic all of the time."

Ruby stared at him, her eyebrows raised, and Dirk looked at her.

"What?" he asked.

"Dirk, the first person I met was Woodruff."

"Ah, right. That would be enough to put anyone in a bad mood." Dirk and Ruby both laughed—the second genuine moment of that day. "That man is…something."

"He is, yes." Ruby paused and was quiet for a moment. She wanted to ask Dirk about Mara, if he had been the squire that helped her on her quest, but she wasn't sure if it was something that should be brought up. She didn't want to upset him, whether that was by knowing about Mara, or by wondering if he was the one with her, because if he was, it meant that he had watched her die.

Ruby shook herself out of her head. Instead of thinking, she moved up next to Dirk, who sat at the very front of the wagon, and she watched as the base of the mountains drew closer. It was strange to her how such a large piece of the earth that looked otherworldly was something they could actually reach. It seemed like it was impossible, like it was some sort of backdrop to the world, and yet, they could climb it.

Again, vague feelings of familiarity entered her mind. It was as if she'd been on this road before, like she'd headed up to these mountains in the past, but just like every other time she tried to remember, she couldn't place the memory.

It seemed like mere moments had passed when they reached the base of the mountain.

"We'll stop here," Dirk said, pulling the horse to a halt. The horse began to graze, and Dirk moved toward the back of the wagon to gather up the supplies they had brought with them.

"We're just going to leave him all tied up like that?" Ruby asked. It looked like the weight of the bars that sat across the horse's back were hurting him.

Dirk looked around and grabbed a rope. "You could tie him to a tree to give him better range."

Ruby nodded and took the rope. She hopped out of the wagon and undid the horse's attachments. He may have been old, with a graying muzzle and slow gait, but his coat was beautiful. It was pure black and shiny. His mane and tail were both long with a bit of a natural wave.

After Ruby loosely tied him to a nearby tree, she pet his muzzle and looked into his soft eyes. He whinnied, and Ruby smiled.

"He's a Friesian." Dirk had found a patch of grass and was setting up the tent he'd brought. "Used to be a racehorse, one of the finest in all of the kingdoms. He outlived all of his riders, which is incredibly uncommon for a horse, but they all died young, mostly in terrible falls while they were racing. No one had any use for him anymore, so the stable boys that worked at his last barn planned to kill him—they simply didn't have room in such a busy stable. The king's son found him."

"The king's son?" Ruby's eyes went wide.

"Channing." Dirk smiled and nodded, as though he was lost in a memory. "He was one of the best-known riders everywhere, and not only because he was the prince, but because he was an incredible rider. He happened to be at the stable taking care of his prized steed when he saw the boys, one of them with a sword in hand. Channing stopped them, resolved to take the horse in as his own, and named him

Sailor. After Channing died, the king couldn't bear to be rid of his son's horse."

Ruby walked over to Dirk and helped him put up the tent. "Is it true that Channing was killed at the market?"

"You're getting your memories back!"

It was a question, but the excitement in Dirk's voice made it sound more like a declaration.

Ruby shook her head sadly. "No, I'm not. One of the other prisoners told me about Mara."

"Mara," Dirk muttered. "Everyone says she was the one to kill the king's son. People even claim they were there to see it, but I don't believe any of them. Mara was sweet and kind, just like Channing. She came to the palace often, despite the king's wishes, and they were wonderful together."

"Didn't they fight?"

"No. They stopped talking for a time because Channing was busy preparing to take over the throne as his father grew older, but they never would have yelled at each other or even harmed the other. I knew both of them well—Mara was my sister, and Channing was my best friend."

"Oh." Ruby knew that she had been right to not ask Dirk about Mara. She was glad she had waited.

"She didn't kill him, I'm certain of that. I wanted to help her, to get the truth from her, but the king forbade me from seeing her after she was locked up. I wasn't allowed to help her during her mission, and she was killed." Dirk paused when his voice cracked and took a deep breath before continuing. "The king kept me on a tight leash because he knew I was close to both of them. He no longer trusts me, but I know he knows Mara didn't kill his son. I don't know how, but I intend to find out."

"If you're a knight, you're closer to the king," Ruby realized.

Dirk looked at her when they had finished setting up the tent. "I just told you all of that," he realized out loud.

Ruby couldn't help but laugh. "Yes, you did."

Desperation covered Dirk's face, and he grabbed Ruby by the shoulders. His brown eyes were the most serious Ruby had ever seen them. "You cannot speak a word of this to anyone."

"I bet you're hoping I die now, so that you don't have to stress about me," Ruby joked, but when Dirk didn't say anything, the mirth left her eyes. "I assure you; my lips are sealed."

"Thank you." Dirk grabbed blankets from the wagon and one of the canteens of water.

"Can I tell you something?" Ruby asked. "A secret for a secret?"

"Of course." Dirk went into the tent, and Ruby followed. "What is it?"

"I think my memories were purposefully taken from me."

Dirk laughed. "I know that."

"You do?" Ruby couldn't hide the hurt in her voice.

He sighed. "I wish I could tell you more, but as I said, the king doesn't trust me. I don't know why he took your memories away, truly."

"Okay." Ruby believed him, and a few moments later, a new idea popped into her head. "What if it has something to do with Channing?" Dirk looked at her, and his eyes widened. "What if I knew something about his death?"

"You weren't friends with him or Mara. Or me, for that matter. I know that for sure, because I've never seen you before."

"But it would explain why he took my memories away. Maybe we weren't friends, but maybe I was there when he died…wrong place, wrong time, you know? Why would the king take my memories, unless he didn't want me to know something?"

"Maybe, but Ruby, you're getting distracted. You cannot be focused on Channing's death right now! You have to focus on this quest. I shouldn't have said anything about Mara, and for that, I apologize, because I know it's still on your mind, and probably will continue to be, but listen to me, Ruby. You *have* to focus."

She shrugged. "I don't think it'll be difficult to focus when I'm facing a giant dragon."

"That may not be the only thing you're facing." Dirk swallowed. "We may come across some dwarves tomorrow."

"How bad can a couple of dwarves be?" Ruby scoffed.

"Oh, they're mean creatures. They may be shorter than us, but all of them have a lot of muscle to them, and these mountains are full of them."

"So? I beat a half-orc. They can't be that difficult."

"Don't let your confidence kill you," Dirk warned again. Then, he smiled. "Maybe it'll be good for you to face some dwarves. Maybe you'll learn your lesson, so long as you don't die."

Ruby rolled her eyes, and Dirk noticed. "You're not listening to me, are you?"

"No," Ruby lied.

Dirk sighed. "You don't understand. They have some sort of deal with the dragon on the mountains. I don't know how it started, but the dwarves love the dragon. It ignites their furnaces and keeps them warm when the mountains get particularly cold. In exchange, they trade it gold, which keeps the baby dragons entertained."

"Really, is that why they like gold?" Ruby asked. Snatches came to her, of the bearded man she knew to be her father, enchanting her with tales of dragons and their ever-increasing hoard of treasure.

Dirk shrugged. "I don't know. I suppose it's shiny, so they like that, and soft enough for them to chew on and sleep on, but that's not the point. The dwarves would protect that dragon with their lives, because, in a way, the dragon is the source of their lives. None of them would be able to survive in the mountains without it."

"Well, I've got nothing to lose," Ruby said. "I don't have my memories. I'd like to survive this and get them back, of course, but if I can't do that without killing some dwarves, then you had better believe I'll fight with everything I have. I'll win this." She saw the uncertain look on Dirk's face. "You don't believe I can do this, do you?"

"No, I do!" Dirk said, a little too enthusiastically. "I just think we have to go up there with a plan in case we do run into any dwarves." Ruby got to her feet and left the tent. "Where are you going?" Dirk called after her.

"I think I'll sleep in the wagon," Ruby muttered.

"Don't be ridiculous! What if it rains?" Dirk's head poked out of the tent. Ruby looked up at the clear sky pointedly. "The wagon isn't even that comfortable. You need the best sleep you can get."

"If you want me to be at my best tomorrow, then leave me alone. You've brought my confidence down enough." Ruby kept walking, and Dirk didn't say anything else.

He'd been right about the wagon not being all that comfortable to sleep in. She tossed and turned as uneven bits of wood jabbed at her back, and she was sure she would have splinters tomorrow, but she didn't care. She huddled up in one of the blankets that was still stacked on the sack of food they had, and she drifted into a fitful sleep.

Every one of her dreams was full of dragons, dwarves, and Dirk. Every time she shifted, her foot bumped against the side of the wagon, and when she'd had enough of it, she left the wagon to sleep on the grass.

For a while, it was rather nice. The mountains looked like a painting under such an infinite sky, and the stars glittered peacefully, making false promises that everything would be alright for Ruby. She almost believed it and started to drift off on the cool grass. She did fall asleep, but she was startled awake by the loud crickets that chirped nearby.

Finally, when the feeling of something crawling on her leg scared her enough, she ducked into the tent. Dirk was asleep, but he opened his eyes when Ruby came in.

"You're back," he murmured quietly, though Ruby could tell that he was far from fully awake.

"Yeah," she whispered, laying down and rolling over to her side, facing away from him. She hadn't wanted him to know she'd returned. Her plan had been to sneak out before Dirk woke up and make him think she'd spent the night in the wagon, but she hadn't accounted for the possibility that he would be a light sleeper.

She heard him move closer to her and tensed when he draped his arm carelessly over her shoulders, just for a brief moment. Ruby assumed it was because he seemed to still be mostly asleep, and he didn't know what he was doing, but he spoke clearly enough.

"You'll finish this quest alive," he promised softly. "I know it."

He turned away, and Ruby almost asked him to come back—the warmth of his body was something she hadn't known she would crave, but she said nothing. For all she knew, he wouldn't remember what he'd done in the morning, and he would be better off for it.

She ignored her thoughts and shut her eyes. Sleep turned out to be elusive, and she still missed the heat of Dirk's arm around her shoulders. She'd thought she was warm with just her blanket, but now, she knew that it wasn't true.

Ruby tried to focus on the mission, on how she really did

need sleep if she was to fight her best tomorrow, but everything led back to either Dirk or the possibility of dying, neither of which were particularly helpful.

She thought of the stars instead and pictured them above her head. She willed herself to sleep by imagining her memories being returned, of her returning to the kingdom with the dragon scales in hand. They were all happy thoughts that seemed incredibly far from reach, but still, Ruby focused on them until she was so close to sleep that she could believe it.

Finally, it washed over her, and there were no dreams, only peaceful darkness.

SAILOR

$\mathcal{T}$he sun rose, and Ruby was the first to wake.

She stretched out her sore back and stepped outside of the tent for a breath of fresh air. She greeted Sailor with some apples she had picked from an apple tree she noticed the previous night when she'd tried to sleep outside. His ears perked up, and he stamped in excitement. Ruby untied him, just for a while, to let him roam freely.

"What are you doing?"

Ruby turned to see Dirk emerging from the tent.

"Letting Sailor walk free for a little bit," she answered. The tips of her ears started to burn when she wondered if Dirk remembered last night. "It's not like he can run away on those old legs."

"Ruby, if anything goes wrong on this mission, even the smallest thing…"

"Stop worrying," she interrupted. "I'll keep an eye on him." Ruby offered Dirk an apple. "Want one?"

He used some of the canteen water to wash it off and took a bite.

"These are pretty good."

"Yeah," Ruby said, munching on a slice of bread that they'd brought with them. Silence hung in the air.

"Do you feel ready for today?" Dirk asked with caution.

"Stop worrying, you'd think that I'm about to spontaneously combust or something." Ruby nudged him with her shoulder. Again, she felt something rush through her at the feeling of his skin on hers. "I feel as ready as someone can be before they're about to stare death in the eyes."

Dirk laughed, but it was just a little bit too loud for Ruby to believe that it was genuine.

"Understandable."

After they finished their food, and Ruby tied Sailor back up to the wagon, they followed a well-traveled trail through the woods. It got steeper and steeper to the point where Sailor was panting and noticeably slowing.

"Maybe we should go on foot from here," Ruby suggested.

"We'd tire out too quickly. Besides, dwarves are more likely to get us if we aren't protected. They don't like horses all that much—not even old ones."

"Wouldn't they be more likely to attack if we're in the wagon, since we're more noticeable?" Ruby asked. "Sailor's not going to be able to go on much longer, and we don't want the king's precious memory of his son dropping dead, do we?"

"Okay, you've got a fair point," Dirk said with a sigh, "but what if Sailor gets attacked while we're gone?"

"We'll just…" Ruby trailed off. She hadn't really thought her plan through. "We'll take him with us," she decided, "and stop whenever he needs to stop, which should be much less frequently without the heavy wagon and us inside it."

"Alright," Dirk agreed. Ruby could tell that he didn't like the plan, but there wasn't anything else they could do. "You better put your armor on, then, unless you want to carry it."

"Oh, yeah." Ruby had started to sweat when she was

outside in front of the tent, and she worried about how hot it would be in her armor. When she suited up, though, she found that it wasn't as bad as she'd feared—there was a pocket of cool air underneath the armor. "Okay, this isn't so bad."

"This would be a good time for a spot of training," Dirk declared, glancing around him. An open meadow surrounded them, and a gentle breeze stirred the mountain flowers that were only now beginning to blossom. He rummaged in the wagon for a moment before tossing her a heater shield. "Catch."

Ruby blinked, but she snatched the big shield out of the air. Before she'd fully realized what she was doing, she had already strapped it to her left arm and drawn a longsword in her right. Dirk stepped forward with similar gear but didn't immediately jump in.

"This feels natural," Ruby commented, raising her shield and gazing over the embossed edge at her squire. "I prefer using my spear, but I must have been trained in this style of fighting as well. Like you, I suppose."

He nodded, then slashed forward, the point of his sword easily deflected by Ruby's heater shield. Dirk jerked back before Ruby could counterattack.

"But you're not from Torbek," he added.

"Could I be Friesian like old Sailor?"

Dirk grinned, sidestepping as he looked for a weak spot. "I doubt it. You're too…" he jabbed forward, nearly hitting Ruby's left knee, but she dodged aside at once before swinging wildly at him. "Hot-blooded," he concluded, dancing back a pace.

"I'll show you hot-blooded," Ruby growled, dashing in with wild abandon. She swung twice, knocking wooden fragments off Dirk's heater shield, before lurching forward and slamming the rim of her own shield into his helmet. He squawked even as he stumbled backward. Ruby felt a rush of delight at her success, and then it was swiftly followed by guilt at harming Dirk. "Are you okay?" she stammered, lowering her sword and shield.

At once Dirk charged back, and it was all she could do to grip his longsword, stepping back a pace. She felt his hot breath on her even through the helmet, and was abruptly hauled to the side, her squire falling atop her.

"Oh, sorry," he muttered, blinking from atop her. Her heartbeat raced, but it wasn't from the exertion. For a long moment they stared into each other's eyes. Then he pushed himself up to his feet and extended a hand. After a few seconds Ruby reached for it, and Dirk hauled her up. Together they stood there, the silence now awkward, and they gathered their wits about them.

"Sailor's eating well," Ruby finally commented, gesturing over at the old horse, who had moved past a few nettles to crop at the grass.

"Uh, yeah," Dirk agreed, then stripped off his heater shield and tossed it back into the wagon. "That was a good practice session."

"It was," Ruby agreed, grateful that her helmet hid her blushing face. "But we should be going now."

"Agreed," Dirk said, gathering up the food and water with one hand and Sailor's reins with the other.

Sailor's strength faded frequently, so they stopped often, always amidst a cluster of trees that would hide them from any caves that might house dwarves. A few times, Ruby thought she heard them passing right by her and Dirk, but she didn't dare peek from behind the trees. Sailor was easier to hide than she'd thought—he laid down to rest, and his black coat blended in well with the surroundings.

They made better progress than Ruby would have

thought. By the time the sun was at its highest point in the sky, they were more than halfway up the mountain.

"This is going well," Ruby said as they walked.

"Don't jinx it!" Dirk snapped, and Ruby rolled her eyes. "I'm serious."

"The outcome of our situation most definitely does not depend on my commentary," Ruby argued.

"You're right. It depends on how loud you are."

Ruby and Dirk both jumped at the new voice behind them. They turned to face its owner, and Ruby already had her spear in hand. Dirk drew his sword behind her.

He had been right about dwarves. The man in front of Ruby was shorter than her, but his muscles were twice as big as hers and Dirk's combined. He spit out a blade of grass he'd been chewing on and rested a meaty hand on an ugly-looking axe.

Others came out behind the dwarf, who Ruby assumed was the leader of the group, and he talked some more. "We've been following you for a while now, and we know you're after our dragon. Get them!"

Sailor ran off into the forest as soon as the dwarves charged at Ruby and Dirk. He was slow, but the dwarves let him get away. Ruby would have been worried about Sailor if she didn't have to worry about herself at that moment.

Three dwarves simultaneously ran for her. Not knowing what else to do, Ruby threw her spear at one of the dwarves, lodging it in his skull. Ruby spent the rest of her time dodging the other two, but more were coming after her, so she used the same move she'd used on Dirk earlier and charged at the ones blocking her from her spear. At the last moment, she ducked her head, rolled into a ball and prayed to the stars that their weapons wouldn't penetrate through her armor.

They didn't, but just as Ruby started to reach for her

spear, the leader stepped hard on her arm. The pressure made her wince, but it wasn't as painful as it would have been if she hadn't been wearing armor.

"It's over," the dwarf said. "You've lost."

Ruby struggled to reach for her spear, even as the dwarf snatched it off the ground and stepped harder on her arm. She looked back and found that Dirk was on his feet, but his own sword was pressed to his neck.

"We'll take you to our cavern and decide your fate there," the dwarf leader said, "though it's more than likely you'll end up dead for disrespecting our god."

"Your god?" Ruby asked, and the dwarf leader started towards her. She flinched backwards.

"The dragon you disrespected by coming here on a mission to slaughter him." The dwarf leader pulled Ruby to her feet, and a few of the other dwarves wrapped her hands in rope. That was how both she and Dirk were brought to the home of the dwarves—leashed like pets.

It was dim inside the cavern, though torches were strung along the curved walls. A pile of animal bones sat to one side, and a pile of fresh meat was on the other. There were prison cells lined up on the sides of the cavern, not unlike the one Ruby woke up in previously.

She and Dirk were thrown into the same cell, even though the other few were empty. The dwarf leader glared at them before heading deeper into the cavern. One was left behind to guard Ruby and Dirk, though he didn't seem very pleased about it.

"I did not leave that rotting cell just to end up in another one," Ruby snarled, rising to her feet and shaking the bars. "Let us out!"

The guard dwarf clanged Ruby's spear against the bars. "Quiet, or next time, it'll go through your neck!"

Ruby backed away and glared daggers at him.

Dirk, who still stood in the middle of the cell, looked over at her with a smirk. "Where's all that confidence?"

"Gone," Ruby muttered. The joke, if it even was a joke, wasn't funny to her anymore. She wanted to survive, but she seemed to be awful at it.

"Come on, brighten up," Dirk said quietly, moving back to sit next to her. Ruby raised an eyebrow. "We'll be fine. I've dealt with dwarves before."

"Oh, really?" Ruby asked, and Dirk pressed a finger to her lips.

"Talk quietly!"

"What are you doing?" Ruby slapped his hand away. The guard dwarf turned to look back at them, confusion and the tiniest hint of concern on his face.

"Just trust me, will you?" Dirk asked, still speaking quietly. "Hush."

"Okay, fine," Ruby said in a whisper. "Now, tell me about these other dwarves you've dealt with."

"Gladly." Dirk smiled again. Ruby started to wonder if he was hiding something, but she didn't question him. "One of my other, less important missions had been to kill some dwarves at the base of this very mountain. This was during the dwarf rebellion, when they wanted the mountains to be recognized as a dwarven kingdom. They got closer to the forest, so I went with a bunch of other men and women working for the king to kill them off. It was difficult, but we overwhelmed them with our numbers and won easily. We threatened the dwarf who had proclaimed himself king. We were given orders to allow him to live, so long as he bowed when the true king came to the mountains, and the dwarf complied. So, they've lived under the king's rule since then, probably angry at us the entire time, but they no longer have the numbers necessary to overtake us. However, that isn't the point of the story."

"Can you get to the point, then?"

"Not a lot of people know this about dwarves, but it takes a great deal of emotion to stir them. Dwarves spend all of their anger and rage in one battle, whether it's a fight with humans or a fight amongst themselves. Once that anger is spent, they tend to drink and sleep to refill it, and you know what? Our guard seemed a little too angry that he was left here to guard us while the dwarf leader brought everyone else back into the cavern." Dirk nodded his head at the guard, whose head was resting against the bars. He was holding Ruby's spear loosely, and she could hear him snoring.

"So?" Ruby asked, deep in thought. "How do we get out?"

"Like this." Dirk pulled a small lock pick out of his pocket. "Dwarves are also stupid. They don't bother searching for things to confiscate. They just take what's obvious, like swords and spears."

"Dirk, you're a lifesaver. Literally. I could kiss you right now!"

The words went flying from Ruby's mouth before she knew what she was saying, and Dirk pressed his hand to her mouth, effectively shushing her again.

"Yeah, um, let's get out of here. We can talk about kissing later," Dirk said, and he, too, seemed to immediately regret his words.

Silently, Dirk brought his lock pick up to the bars and dug around in the lock. Ruby could tell it was difficult to both move the pick around and to avoid the sleeping guard's head, but Dirk managed, and the door creaked open.

Ruby rushed out and carefully took her spear from the guard's slack grip while Dirk searched for his sword. Just as they were leaving the cavern, the dwarf leader approached.

"Hey!" he yelled, stopping Ruby and Dirk in their tracks as well as waking the guard. "The prisoners are escaping!"

He and his men charged at Ruby and Dirk, and they dashed toward the forest.

"We can't fight them off, and if they catch us again, we won't be able to escape so easily," Dirk panted. Ruby understood what he was saying. They had one chance to get away, or they wouldn't survive.

By some stroke of luck, they ran right into Sailor. He was trying to reach an apple in a tree, and though Ruby felt bad, she jumped onto his back. He whinnied and reared back.

"Hey, hey, hey," she whispered, and it seemed to calm him down enough, "it's just us." She helped Dirk up on the old horse's back. He was under a lot of stress, she could tell, but the dwarves were coming, and they were angry.

"Okay," Ruby said, leaning down to stroke a hand over Sailor's mane, "I need you to run. I know you're old and that this is an uphill climb, but we have to get out of here." Ruby squeezed her heels against his side gently, and she was surprised at how fast he took off.

She fell back into Dirk's arms and laughed as Sailor made his way around the dwarves and up towards the peak of the mountain. He only ran long enough for the three of them to get enough of a head start that they could hide deep within the trees nearby. Ruby and Dirk got off the old horse, and even though he was exhausted, it seemed like he had enjoyed the short run.

They stayed quiet, hidden in the branches. Some of the dwarves came into view, running up the twisting path, but they looked tired and ready to give up.

"I don't see them!" Ruby heard one of the men call. He was out of breath.

"Keep looking!"

That was the dwarf leader's voice.

"Why can't we just let the dragon burn them up?"

"What if the dragon takes his rage out on us for letting them get so far? They've got to be here. That horse was old."

They started searching the forest. Ruby's heart pounded so loudly in her chest that she worried the dwarves would hear it. Sailor fell asleep quickly, but his ears twitched every time he heard a sound.

The dwarves didn't search deep enough to find them, and Ruby looked to the side, sending Dirk a quick thumbs up.

"Let's just go home!" one of the dwarves grumbled, turning back. "We were supposed to feast tonight."

"No feast if we don't find them!" the dwarf leader responded. The party of dwarves had gone past where Ruby and Dirk were hiding, but she knew that they would have to wait for the dwarves to go home before they moved.

"They're not here!"

One of the dwarves chased after the leader, and soon, the clearing grew quiet.

"What do we do?" Ruby breathed.

"I don't know," Dirk answered just as quietly.

"We could go deeper?"

"They'd hear us...they have extremely sensitive ears. Besides, Sailor's a dead giveaway if they come back down the mountain. Also, we'd probably get lost. This forest stretches way farther than you'd think, and there are plenty of creatures worse than dwarves in it. We should wait them out and hope with everything we have that they pass us by."

The voices started up again, and the two of them fell into a tense silence. Ruby pressed herself closer to the ground.

"Get back here!" the dwarf leader yelled. "We're not done!"

"Yes, we are!" a different dwarf called back. He and a group of others were storming back down the mountain. With a frustrated sigh, the dwarf leader followed them.

Ruby and Dirk stayed motionless until they knew for

certain that they were in the clear. After a few minutes of silence, they ran up the mountain, coaxing Sailor into a brisk pace.

They didn't dare to slow down until Sailor became too tired to run anymore. Ruby pet his neck repeatedly and scratched his sweaty back in an apology.

"I can't believe we almost got killed by dwarves," Dirk said quietly, as though he was afraid they were still listening.

"It's all part of the quest!" Ruby exclaimed with false cheer. She was tired of the mountains already.

"Well, the good or bad news, depending on how you look at it, is that we're almost at the top of the mountain already."

"Oh, great." Ruby stopped and looked up. They were at the last stretch of mountain, and the sun was just beginning to set. "Can we sleep first? Somewhere out in the forest?"

"I say we kill the dragon and then sleep in its cavern."

"What about the babies?"

"Assuming they're still young, which they should be, they're completely helpless without their mother."

"That just makes me feel bad," Ruby said, crossing her arms. For the first time since the quest had begun, she was questioning her morals. She guessed that being around Sailor had something to do with it.

"Ruby." Dirk put his hands on her shoulders and turned her to face him. "It's your life, or it's the dragon's life. Do you want to feel bad, or do you want to die?"

"Neither," Ruby whined. She hated the way she sounded and snapped herself out of it. For a while, she just paced back and forth, trying to mentally prepare herself for this, but she didn't know if it was possible to be mentally prepared to kill a dragon. A mother dragon, at that.

"You've got to pick, and if you kill the dragon tonight, we have plenty of time to get back."

"Then I could mull it over for a day or so."

"Being up here is dangerous, especially with Sailor. Come on, you've got this," Dirk promised.

"You're just saying that so I stop wasting time."

Dirk didn't even try to hide it. "That is part of it, yes. Now, I really believe that you can do this. You already told me your strategy, and I think it'll work."

"I'm scared," Ruby admitted, and it felt like her heart was weightless. It had been laying heavy inside of her as an insidious, creeping thing, and now, it was gone in two simple words.

"Who wouldn't be?" Dirk asked. "Listen, if you want those answers, you had better go kill that dragon and ensure that you get the scales. If I thought you couldn't do it, I'd be telling you that you aren't ready. I've grown rather fond of you over this journey, and I am telling you that you can do this."

Ruby nodded, more to reassure herself than because she actually believed him. She understood then what he and the prisoner had meant when they'd said her confidence would kill her. If she had faced the dragon with all of her worries still bottled up inside, she wouldn't have been able to think clearly enough to slay the dragon.

It had taken a journey up the mountain and being locked up in a dwarf's cavern, but now, she was ready.

IN THE END

*I*n the end, when Ruby got to the cavern ready to face the dragon, she found that it was gone. She crept inside, searching for any sign of the creature, but it was clearly empty except for the nest at the back. Ruby didn't see anything inside of the nest, but she didn't want to get close enough for a curled-up dragon baby to breathe fire in her face.

She was disappointed when she returned to Dirk, where he waited in the forest. Ruby frowned as she trudged down the path, her newfound confidence already wavering.

"The dragon wasn't there," she told Dirk when she crept behind the thick brush.

"Dragons don't usually hunt at night," Dirk mused. "That's strange. Maybe there's a food shortage, and she's working double time."

"Maybe," Ruby said. She could feel the adrenaline fading, and suddenly, her limbs wereheavy with exhaustion.

Dirk seemed to notice.

"Hey," he said softly, "you had it in you tonight, and you'll have it in you again tomorrow."

"I don't think I can sleep tonight," Ruby sighed, staring at the soft grass. "I think I'll have nightmares and wake up too much. I'd rather just stay awake."

"Are you sure?"

"Yes."

"Okay." Dirk paused and laid a gentle hand on her arm. "Let me come with you tomorrow."

"What?"

"Let me face the dragon with you. This is also my quest, and I don't want to just sit here while you do the hard part."

"Dirk, no. You need to stay with Sailor, and if anything goes wrong, you're supposed to make it out alive. The armor, remember?" Ruby asked with a smile.

"I don't care about the armor!"

The words burst out of Dirk, and he quieted down, a flush of red under his cheeks. "All I'm saying is that I don't think it's fair for you to face this alone."

"Well, it wasn't fair that I lost my memories, nor was it fair for me to be forced to fight that half-orc, but here I am," Ruby said with a snort.

"That's what I'm saying, Ruby. You've already gone through enough alone, so let me help you with this."

"No. This is my quest to finish. Your task is only to accompany me, and you've done that. I know you don't want to, but let me do this alone." Ruby took his hand and gave it a quick squeeze.

He nodded reluctantly and looked down at the grass. "Okay, you're right, but if you need help, I'll go in there the moment you call for it, got it?"

"Got it. I promise to yell if I need anything."

"And you really should try to get some rest." Dirk's fingers picked at the grass. "Today has been…a lot. You'll be drained tomorrow, and if you have nightmares tonight, just remember that I'm here. I would never let anything bad happen to you."

Ruby just stared at him for a moment—it was all she could do, and he looked up at her.

"Thank you," she said. She laid down and took Dirk's advice. She closed her eyes, but once more, her dreams were full of too many horrible things for her to get peaceful, reenergizing sleep. She saw faceless shadows that screamed at her to remember them, but she couldn't. She was back in the arena with the half-orc, but it felt as if she was moving through quicksand, while the half-orc could dart from one corner of the arena to the other. She saw the dwarves surrounding her, their yells telling of her impending failure, and finally, as she lay bleeding on the ground, she saw fire exploding from a dragon's mouth, killing them all. It roared at her and opened its jaws wider and wider. Ruby could feel her skin tightening from the heat, when suddenly, she was shaken awake.

"Ruby!"

She woke to Dirk shaking her shoulders gently, though she didn't recognize that at first. She balled her hands into fists, her eyes wide open, and Dirk slowly pressed her arms down to the ground.

"You were kicking and yelling," he murmured.

"Nightmares," she said as if he hadn't already figured it out. She'd fallen asleep early, and as she blearily looked around, Ruby realized that she was sleeping in a tent. She hadn't even known he'd brought it with him. "Did you set this up?"

"Yes," he said, and even though he didn't say more, she found herself wondering if he had carried her inside. "Now, come here."

"What?" Ruby asked, turning to look at him.

He stretched out an arm. "Lay with me," he gestured at

the empty spot next to him. "Maybe if you're next to me, you'll sleep more peacefully."

"Maybe," Ruby said. She hesitated a moment, and then lay down beside him. "Do you think anyone's looking for me?" she blurted out. "Could I have family somewhere out there, I mean?"

Dirk frowned beside her. "You mean a husband?"

"No!" Ruby said with a chuckle. "Definitely not. I can tell that at least."

"Right," Dirk agreed with a slight smile.

"But I feel like sometimes I get the briefest flashes of memories," Ruby continued. "Like a vague sense of my mother being there and the smell of baking bread, and crashing waves with the tang of sea salt. And my father... though I can't make him out exactly, I know he was tall and had a thick beard. But why is that all I remember?"

"Maybe the memories that come back earliest are the strongest ones," Dirk mused, as Ruby moved into his arms and buried her face against his chest. He wrapped his arms loosely around her back, and she melted into his comforting embrace. "Of course you'd start to remember your parents first," he continued. "So you're on the right track! Maybe other vivid memories will come back to you soon."

"I hope I remember this," Ruby murmured softly, and they fell into a pleasant silence as the night fell around them. She felt like she wanted to stay there forever with him. Being with him made her realize how lonely she was before.

Even though she felt awkward, sprawled out the way she was, she was comfortable. Ruby listened to Dirk's heartbeat and was surprised at how loud it was. Closing her eyes, she let the rhythmic thump of his heart carry her off into a blank, peaceful sleep.

A memory came to her in her dreams: a crackling fire and a scratchy sensation above. She craned her neck up to see a thick thatch of beard, and she heard her mother chuckle at something. "And what else do you know about dragons?" a boy's voice asked excitedly. His eyes shone in the firelight.

My brother!

"There's a legend about the little ones," her father's voice boomed out from above her. "That they're not completely immune to fire. They have scales, to be sure, but they have a long way to go, just like you and Ruby…"

When she woke, she truly did feel rested, and Dirk was already awake.

"These are our last couple pieces of bread," he said, handing a piece to her.

"Thanks." Ruby took it and ate quietly, unable to stop thinking about how it felt to be held last night. She still felt bubbly and found herself excited for the next night, hoping they'd still be on the road, and he could hold her one more time before they returned.

But questions about the future flew into her mind uninvited. When her memories returned, would she stay in the same wretched kingdom just to be with Dirk? Did he even want to be with her, or was he just doing all he could to help her through this quest by making her comfortable? Did she actually want to be with him, or was she just hungry for companionship?

"Do you know if the dragon returned last night?" Ruby asked, trying to get all of the questions out of her head. She hurried to get her armor on—she didn't want to have time to be afraid, she just wanted to get her last quest over with.

"I heard wingbeats in the middle of the night, and it sounded far too large to be a bird. I believe she's back."

"Good."

When Ruby finished with her armor, she grabbed her spear and rooted through her pack to find an apple for Sailor, who was tied to a tree once more.

"You're going now," Dirk stated, and Ruby wondered if he meant it as a question.

"Yes. We've...I've got to finish this."

"Good luck." Dirk put a hand on each of her shoulders, and Ruby looked up at him.

"Thank you," she whispered before pulling away and hurrying up to the dragon's cavern. She could feel Dirk's eyes on her back.

Realizing that he was something else to fight for, Ruby clutched her spear in her sweaty hands and focused only on moving her feet rather than facing the dragon. The best mindset she could be in was one where she wasn't over-thinking everything.

In front of her, the mouth of the cavern yawned open, and somehow, even in the early morning light, it seemed darker than it had last evening. She realized that it was because of the dragon that was curled up in the cave. Black lines on the creature's great head showed that she was asleep, but Ruby didn't doubt the mother dragon would hear her creep in. She had to rush into this and get a blow in before the dragon was fully awake.

So, Ruby did. She charged at the dragon, who opened an eye and raised her head, but not before Ruby managed to lodge her spear in its chest. Immediately, the dragon roared and spit fire right where Ruby had been just seconds ago. The dragon's scales shimmered under the flames, and it was clearly immune to its own fire.

The dragon stood and let out an ear-piercing shriek. Pushing her wings down, she buffeted Ruby with great gusts of wind, and the dragon's endless stream of fire roared in Ruby's ears. She ducked behind a protruding piece of rock, and the edges of her armor started to melt. Terror coursed through Ruby's body—this armor wasn't enough to protect her. She had to end this quickly, but she didn't know how.

Then, Ruby had an idea. When the dragon stopped to take a breath, Ruby raced towards the back of the cavern where she'd seen the nest.

She just had to hope that there actually were baby dragons, and that they were young enough to not have developed any resistance to fire yet.

Ruby dove behind the nest and was relieved to see that the mother had closed her jaws. When Ruby peered into the nest, sure enough, there were three tiny babies, their eyes barely open. The mother slithered towards Ruby, and in a rush of panic, Ruby grabbed one of the babies and held her spear to it. It cried and struggled, and its pitiful whines grated on her conscience.

Dragons were intelligent. They knew what pain a blade could bring, and the bond they shared with their babies went deeper than any other creature's. When the mother understood that Ruby was threatening her, she pressed herself to the ground, her jaws still shut and her wings flat on the cavern floor. She exposed her chest where a solid red mass glowed from inside of it—the dragon's heart.

She was willing to lay down her life to keep her babies alive. Whatever Ruby had been expecting, however she had thought she'd have to fight...everything fell away in that moment.

The baby was still crying, and the others in the nest had started to let out their own cries of alarm. Ruby knew she couldn't kill their mother, but she also knew that the king could trick her or tell her she did not complete the quest correctly by leaving the dragon alive. War raged in Ruby's mind as a mother waited to die and a baby cried to live— every noise from the little one's jaws tugged at Ruby's heart.

Ruby didn't have time to make a decision. She let the baby go, and the mother opened one of her big eyes. Ruby stopped, waiting for her to burn her to a crisp now that she was away from the mother's babies, but she didn't—she just watched Ruby.

"I'm sorry," Ruby whispered. She pressed the blade of the spear onto the mother's scales where her heart was and closed her eyes. Still, she could not bring herself to kill such a magnificent beast. Her arms wouldn't move.

Instead, she lodged the tip of her spear under one of the mother's scales. The dragon roared in pain, and Ruby quickly pried away a few more until five scales laid at her feet. Ruby gathered them up and backed away from the mother, who seemed to understand that Ruby only needed the scales.

Ruby ran down the mountain when she had them in her grasp. She almost didn't want to go straight to where Dirk was waiting because she was trembling so much and didn't quite trust herself to stay on her feet. The idea that she'd done it, that she'd finished her quest, didn't yet seem real to her, and Dirk, too, had a look of shock on his face.

"I heard roaring," Dirk said, "and then there was nothing."

"I got the scales." Ruby showed them to him. Each one was slightly bigger than the palm of her hand, and they were beautiful. She'd thought the dragon to be black at first, but in the morning sun, the scales glinted a deep red. "I didn't kill her, Dirk. I couldn't do it…she had babies."

"Ruby…" Dirk stared at the scales. "The king is going to know."

"My quest was to get the scales, not to kill the dragon. He'll accept this—he has to."

"Listen to me, you can't mess up this quest. You can't do anything that strays even the slightest bit from what the king asked of you. Your life hangs in the balance."

"I won't do it, Dirk. I won't." Ruby had made up her mind, and there was no changing it.

"What if he kills you anyways?" Dirk asked.

"Then I'll die knowing I did the right thing." Ruby took

her armor off and stared at the melted parts of it on the edges while Dirk got Sailor's rope off and put his reins on. Dirk didn't say anything else as they returned down the mountain.

Ruby wanted to race down on Sailor's back as quickly as she could. She didn't want to have to chance of running into dwarves again, but she didn't want to tire Sailor out, either, so they walked back down.

She reached up and ran her fingers over her headdress. It was starting to give her a headache, and she would be glad to have it off when she returned. Even though there could still be danger ahead, Ruby felt an immense weight lifted off her chest. She'd completed her quest without having to kill any dragons, and she was on her way to get her memories back.

The same questions crept back into her mind, but they were interrupted by ambushers suddenly jumping out of the bushes and trees around Ruby, Sailor, and Dirk. Dirk fell backwards in surprise, and his shoulders slid over the ledge. This part of the path was narrow—it was probably the worst place to fight off dwarves.

Still, they didn't have any other choice. Dirk was quickly overwhelmed, and Ruby tried to get to him, but two dwarves charged toward her. She fought hard, but there were just too many.

Suddenly, the dwarf leader stood in front of her, and with a yell, he swung his axe down to where her head had just been.

"Stop!" she yelled. "I didn't kill the dragon, I swear!"

"You hold her scales!" he snarled, readying his axe again, and Ruby tried to move out of the way, but there were other dwarves keeping her where she was.

"I took them without killing her! Let me go, and I'll leave in peace! Please, I just need the scales!"

"For what?" the dwarf leader asked suspiciously.

"The king," Ruby confessed, and as she saw the dwarf's axe descend, she decided to plead one more time. "Wait! Hear me out, please!"

The dwarf leader looked at his men and seemed to be silently communicating with them.

He turned to Ruby and nodded. "Fine, I will let you explain yourself."

Ruby took a deep breath and chose her words carefully in her mind, but the dwarf leader seemed to be getting impatient, so she spoke. "I woke up in a prison cell without my memories. A man came to me and told me I had to face a half-orc for murdering an individual in the king's court. I won. My second quest was to come here and take five dragon scales. I was promised that my memories would be returned to me if I did this."

"You killed one of the king's men, did you?" the dwarf leader asked with a smile.

"Yes," Ruby said, though she knew that it was all a lie, "and I realized I didn't have to kill the dragon. I didn't want to, so I took her scales and left."

"You expect me to believe she just let you?"

"Actually, yes. When I took cover behind her babies so that she wouldn't breathe fire at them, she gave up and laid down. She didn't want me to hurt them—she was ready to give her own life for them. Instead, I took her scales and left. She's okay."

The dwarf leader cast a pensive gaze over her, and he seemed to be deep in thought. Ruby was sure he would kill her anyways, just for the trouble she'd caused him, but instead, he nodded.

"Very well. I can still feel her presence here. I know you're telling the truth, and I believe you when you say you are not a willing part of the kingdom that tried to destroy us. As for him," the dwarf leader said, nodding towards where

Dirk was still pinned down against the ledge, "I recognize him."

"He's changed," Ruby pleaded as she sat up and got to her feet. "He's on my side."

"That doesn't bring back all of the dwarves he murdered."

The dwarf leader walked over to Dirk and spit at his feet.

"Please, don't hurt him!" Ruby ran after the dwarf leader and grabbed his arm, but he turned, a threat burning in his eyes.

"I've spared your life, girl. Don't push your luck."

The dwarf leader looked back at Dirk even though he was still speaking to Ruby. "You have two choices: you can walk away with your life and your dragon scales under my mercy. You can return to that kingdom and get your memories back, but you leave him behind. Your second option is to stay and choose his side, the side of the murderous king, and we will kill you both. What will it be?"

A MILLISECOND EARLIER

The moment weighed heavily on her while Dirk yelled at her to leave.

"Ruby, go!" Dirk tried to push against the dwarves that were holding him down, but it did him no good. "You can get your memories back. You can return with the scales and the armor, even if it is a little out of shape." Despite his situation, he smiled at his comment. "You've got your whole life to discover. I deserve punishment for what I did. Please, go before they change their minds!"

"You were supposed to be the one that returned no matter what," Ruby said to him, tears in her eyes. "Not me."

"I've lived my life!" Dirk yelled. "I've gotten to grow up into a man, and I got to meet you. If that isn't enough, then I don't know what is. Just get out of here!"

"You should listen to the boy," the dwarf leader said. His people had backed away from Ruby, giving her a chance to leave, but Ruby didn't have it in her. She couldn't just leave. She had to save him.

Unthinking, she dove towards Dirk, who was standing precariously close to the edge. All she knew was that she had to help him and get him away from the dwarves, but she didn't know how. She just had to get to him.

"Ruby, no!" he yelled, and just before she reached him, the dwarves around him pushed him over the ledge. Ruby reached for his hand, but she was just out of reach. Just another second would have been enough.

For many moments, he fell. And time seemed to slow as Ruby knelt in the dirt, watching him plummet as though there was still something she could do to save him.

His mouth was open in a silent scream. His hands reached up to her, the very hands that she couldn't reach, and she sobbed as she watched his body break on the ground below.

Ruby needed to get to him, but the moment she turned, the dwarf leader grabbed her collar and pulled her down close to his face. He knew she wanted to kill him for what he'd just done.

"You got one last chance to get out of here," he said menacingly, "before we kill you too."

Ruby started forward, then stopped. Dirk wanted her to live her life. He wanted her to get her memories back and figure out who she was. If anything, she needed to live for him.

Instead of fighting, Ruby dipped her head. Her eyes were locked with the dwarf leader's, and he let her go after a long moment.

She looked over the ledge and found Sailor a few paces away. He looked ready to bolt again, but he didn't seem to have it in him.

Before she returned to the cart, she needed to go retrieve Dirk's body. Seeing him was the last thing she wanted to do, when just moments ago, it was all she had wanted. If she could have, she would have left him and chosen to remember him in his life, but what kind of end to his body was that, being left to the scavengers? She needed to bring him back and find his family so that they could bury him properly.

Her footsteps were slow. It wasn't for Sailor; it was for herself. She dreaded seeing him, but she followed the winding trails and found their cart. She attached Sailor to it and took the reins. She was numb as she guided Sailor into the valley. She hated that he was walking the tiniest bit faster with one less life to carry.

As they drew closer, Ruby could make out a heap on the ground. Ruby could barely look at him as she approached, and at first, she thought she'd simply hallucinated his body moving. She thought it was the grief playing tricks on her mind, but when she got down from the cart and started walking, she heard him choking.

She started running and began to wish she'd walked faster down the mountain. Dirk looked horrible: cuts and bruises littered his body under his torn-up shirt and shorts, but he was alive. He was barely breathing, but he was alive.

"Dirk," Ruby said, falling to the ground and touching a gentle hand to his shoulders. "You survived that! I've got to get you back!"

He was too heavy for her to carry, so she slowly dragged him back to the cart, stumbling while she did. A strangled sound escaped Dirk, and he looked as if he wanted to say something, but Ruby put her finger to his lips the same way he had to her. He smiled briefly and let Ruby lay him down without trying to speak anymore.

Quickly, Ruby took Sailor's reins and lashed them down. Sailor snorted and lifted his front hooves in surprise.

"I'm sorry," Ruby apologized, "but we have to go!"

Sailor picked up on her urgency and raced down the same road they'd taken to the mountain. He got tired just as often as when they'd been going the opposite direction, but he kept pushing onwards, faster and faster. Even when the sun had started to sink, he didn't stop, and Ruby, though she had wished many times for a younger, stronger horse, couldn't have been more grateful for Sailor.

She often checked on Dirk as they went on. Most of the time, he was unconscious, but his chest would still rise and fall. Ruby knew he was beyond any normal healing, but magic could still save him.

She wondered if it already had, if it was the reason Dirk had survived a fall that should have killed him. It was the only explanation, that he was protected by magic to ensure his return, and Ruby hoped that it would save him again.

The palace was visible in the distance. She began yelling as she approached, and Sailor slowed. Guards ran up to them, and they didn't seem to recognize her until they spotted both the headdress on her head and Dirk's body in the wagon.

"Get him to Woodruff!" Ruby screamed as the guards picked Dirk's limp body up. "Heal him!"

One of the guards stayed behind. "You were sent to retrieve the dragon scales, correct?" he asked in a monotone voice.

"Yes, I have them," Ruby said breathlessly, jumping out of the wagon. She showed them to the guard, but when he reached for them, Ruby pulled her hand away. "I'll only deliver them to Woodruff."

"You don't make demands around here, prisoner," the guard spat. Ruby wished she had her spear when the guard grabbed her arm, twisting it painfully until she dropped the scales. The guard picked them up and left her there by the wagon. "I will notify Woodruff of your return at once, as soon as I deliver you to your cell."

"I'm not a prisoner anymore! Let me go!" Ruby demanded, trying to get out of the guard's grip. Panic rose in her mind. Had all of this been a trick? Was the king going back on his word?

Ruby was forced through the back door and down the steps to the dungeon. Her eyes took a long time to adjust, and she felt just as wretched as when she'd first woken up in her cell.

The guard shoved her into it and locked the door. He admired and turned the dragon scales over and over in his hand as he retreated. Ruby wanted to demand Woodruff's presence, but she didn't want to prioritize herself over Dirk. Silently, she promised to wait as long as it took for her freedom, as long as he got better.

"You lived," said the same prisoner that had told Ruby about Mara.

"Did Mara really kill Channing?" Ruby demanded.

"Yes, she did. I witnessed it."

"You're lying."

"What?" the prisoner asked, confused. He sounded genuine, but he had to be the one lying—Ruby refused to believe that Dirk would lie to her.

Ruby didn't answer his question. Pacing around her cell, she stayed quiet, too lost in her own racing thoughts.

This wasn't how she had expected her return to the palace to go. She thought she'd be welcomed and praised for completing a quest that none other could, and that her memories would have been given back to her on sight. For some reason, she thought Woodruff would greet her.

But she'd also thought that Dirk would have returned unscathed, and she quickly realized that things never really turned out how she expected.

Her outlook on everything changed as she sat there in that cell for hours, waiting for someone to tell her the truth. Everyone seemed to be lying and breaking their promises. Ironically enough, only the dwarf had kept his promise. And, in a way, so had the dragon. Ruby had made an unspoken deal with her to leave her cavern and never come back so long as the dragon let her leave.

Maybe the villains weren't who she thought they were.

By the time Woodruff came for her, Ruby was more confused than she had been in the beginning.

"You braved the dragon!" he said loudly, and his voice boomed in the dungeon. "You brought back the scales! Oh, how proud of you I am!"

"Did you heal Dirk?" Ruby demanded, not looking up at Woodruff even when she heard her cell door creak open.

"Yes. He is currently in the process of recovery. He will be fine in a few days, maybe a week."

"I want to see him."

"I am sorry, I cannot let you do that," Woodruff said apologetically, mockingly. Ruby felt as if he was making fun of her, but she didn't press him.

"Why am I a prisoner?" she asked next. "I did everything you asked. I did what no one else could, and the first thing that happened to me was that I was thrown down here again. Why?"

"I do apologize for that. With so many guards, sometimes some of them don't receive the correct orders, like to direct you to the king rather than the dungeon." Ruby could feel Woodruff peering at her as though there was something suspicious about her. "Is something wrong? You seem different."

"I've been through hell and back, and I'm exactly where I started!" Ruby yelled, finally looking up. "Your promises were lies, weren't they?"

"They weren't! Not at all! Here, look at this." Woodruff sat next to her on her cot. He held out a golden chalice to her, and she took it, watching as the jewels embedded in it glittered in the candlelight. "I assumed you would have gotten your memories back on your own after some time. I hoped it wouldn't come to magic, because magic can be a very unpredictable thing. Unfortunately, it looks like it must." Woodruff sighed. "You truly don't remember anything?"

"No," Ruby said quietly. "Nothing before waking up here."

"Well, before you drink this, let me get that headdress off your head." Woodruff said. The headdress loosened immediately. He plucked it off and set it in his lap. "Does that feel better? You must be in as good of a mindset as you can be before gaining your memories back."

"Yes," Ruby said with relief. Her head was beginning to clear, and she didn't feel quite so crazy. "Some food and water would help too."

"Unfortunately, you have to drink this on an empty stomach. I assume it's been a while since the last time you ate."

Ruby nodded.

"Good." Woodruff stood and watched her carefully. "I'll stay while you drink it to ensure that it works properly."

Ruby held the chalice to her lips. It smelled wonderful, like grapes and blueberries and many other fruits. A tinge of excitement shot through her veins. This was her solution! This would bring back everything. She would have a family, a home, maybe even friends. The world would finally make sense.

She drank the whole thing as quickly as she could.

"It may make you sleepy, but not to worry. Your memories will return either in your dreams or when you awaken. Magic can be unpredictable. Come. Let me take you to a nicer, more comfortable bed in the palace."

Ruby had to lean on Woodruff as he guided her up the stairs and down many hallways. The magic was definitely working. She could feel the coolness of it seeping through her system.

Woodruff opened a tall door, and Ruby stumbled into a

room that seemed far too big for just one person. There was a giant, round bed in the middle with the same blue as the palace, as well as fluffy white pillows. Around the room were various dressers, wardrobes, and desks. The opulence was overwhelming

"I could definitely get used to this," Ruby said as Woodruff led her to the bed, and she collapsed into it. She didn't know that mattresses could be so soft, and she felt as if she was floating on clouds.

"I'm sure you could." Woodruff put a hand on her shoulder before standing up to leave. Ruby drifted off to sleep, and the last thing she heard was the distinct sound of Woodruff locking the door behind him.

A HINT OF FAMILIARITY

*R*uby opened her eyes, squinting in the pitch black of her room. A pounding headache throbbed in her skull, and she absently rubbed at her forehead. She felt well-rested, but she couldn't shake the feeling that something was wrong.

Quickly realizing that she was being held in a prison cell, Ruby shot upright on her cot, but she froze as footsteps sounded in the corridor outside. The door opened, and a man dressed in a rich purple robe strode in, a bowl of slop in one hand, and a bowl of water in the other.

"How are you feeling today, prisoner?" the man asked, bending down and sliding the bowls through the bars. Her stomach rumbled, and there was an inexplicable twinge of fear inside of her, so instead of answering, she simply ate her food. "Good," the man said with a smile, "you'll need your strength. You have a very long day ahead of you."

Thoughts raced through her head, and she grappled with the vague familiarity to both the man and the prison, but somehow, Ruby couldn't place either of them in her memory.

What was happening to her?

THE LOCKPICK

The man watched as Ruby ate and began to speak of a big event that was planned for the day.

"You suffered a concussion," the man explained, "as a result, your memory is gone. It should come back over time, though, and in the meantime, you must face your punishment."

"For what?" Ruby asked. She couldn't shake the feeling that she'd been here before, had seen this man before. She could feel...something, but she didn't know what it was.

"Why am I in a prison cell?"

"You assaulted a member of the king's court. As a result, and as custom in this kingdom, you will face a half-orc who murdered an innkeeper and his family. You are both murderers, and only one of you will be allowed to live. If you survive, you will go on to complete a quest for the king."

Ruby felt as if she was in a dream. Her head was still fuzzy, and even though she couldn't think clearly, she couldn't shake the feeling that this man was wrong, that her being in a prison cell was wrong. She especially couldn't comprehend that she had murdered someone, though there was some familiarity to the accusation.

"What would I do after facing the half-orc?" Ruby asked, and she tried her best to mask her confusion. She simply listened to the man and moved up to the bars, pressing her body against the cold metal, listening intently to his every word.

The man looked at her with his head tilted like she'd said something wrong. There was poorly hidden disappointment in his voice when he spoke. "I assumed you would be much more talkative," he remarked, "and that you would have made some snarky comment by now."

"You knew me before?" A small bit of hope fluttered in her chest.

"Yes, but only briefly," the man said quickly. He glanced around. "Now, I will leave you to prepare for your upcoming battle. I will return in a few hours to fetch you."

"Okay," Ruby said, backing away from the cell. For a moment, the man only stared at her like he was trying to figure something out, and Ruby pretended to ignore him. She'd finished both of her bowls already and returned to her cot to lay down.

Finally, he left, and Ruby quietly crept back up to the bars. She heard him make a strange remark to one of the two men who had been waiting in the shadows.

"I liked her much more before," the man in purple murmured. "She was…more of a challenge."

Ruby had the feeling that she was onto something. The man wasn't being entirely honest with her, and she intended to find out what was really going on.

She pulled out the little silver object she'd stolen from his pocket and glanced at it to make sure it was what she needed. She was surprised when she found her eyes being pulled back to it instead of focusing on the lock.

The lock pick belonged to someone she had known. Ruby was certain of it. Memories of its owner flashed through her mind, but much like the rest of her memories, they were fuzzy and distorted. She couldn't make out his face, but she felt a mix of affection and grief burst through her mind.

It was difficult to shake her returning emotions, but she had to put them to the side if she was going to escape. Fiddling with the lock was a lot harder than it looked, and it was much more frustrating, but Ruby kept trying. Finally, it clicked, and Ruby easily pushed the door open.

"Let me out!" a voice called from down the row. "Or I'll call for the guards and tell them that you've escaped!"

Ruby hurried to the cell. "Keep your voice down!" she hissed, kneeling and finding herself face to face with an older man. He had a scruffy white beard and a kind face. It was easy to read the desperation in his voice. "I will, but first, tell me what you know about me."

"I will, as soon as we're away from the prison," the man said.

"No! You'll tell me now. You know something, I can see it. You recognize me."

"I really can't tell you."

"Well, then I really can't let you out."

Conflict played across the man's eyes, and he looked around as though he was afraid of being watched.

He sighed. "You have succeeded."

"You're going to have to go into more detail than that."

"You have been sent to complete these quests before," the man insisted, "and you have succeeded, both with the half-orc and the dragon."

"The dragon?" Ruby wanted to press him for more details, but new voices echoed down the hallway. "I'll let you out as soon as they're gone," Ruby promised, rushing back to her cell and closing the door before two guards came into view.

Ruby tried to look casual as she walked back to her cot. She tucked the lock pick into the waistband of her thin cotton pants and laid down. Staring up at the ceiling, she thought about what the man had said.

She'd done these missions before. It should have been an absurd thought, but it was familiar. Ruby knew it was the truth, but what she couldn't understand was why. She wondered if she could get answers out of the purple-robed man.

The guards walked all the way down the length of the prison, even though it seemed that Ruby and the older man were the only two in there. Still, she couldn't help but wonder if there was someone else at the end of the rows. She decided to find out as soon as the guards were gone, and Ruby could leave her cell again.

They walked past her, and she could feel their eyes linger. When they left, they whispered something unintelligible to each other. They were far quieter than the man in the purple robe had been.

When she didn't hear voices anymore, she quietly pushed the door open and silently walked to the older man's cell. She opened his lock the same way she did hers.

"Thank you," he said, and he took off towards the stairs. Ruby started to follow him, but she looked back at the end of the long row of cells. There was someone down there, and she wanted to know who.

The man grabbed her arm. "Let's go! You're wasting time."

"You go," Ruby murmured.

The man followed her gaze. "No, you can't talk to that prisoner—he's dangerous."

"Who is he?"

"An enemy of the king."

"Aren't we all enemies of the king? What did you do to get yourself thrown in a cell, anyway?"

"We can discuss that when we're far away from here." the man tugged on Ruby's arm, but she flung him off and started toward the darkened corner of the prison. Just then, voices returned, two of which were the guards and one that belonged to the man in the purple robe.

"Stop!" he yelled after Ruby, and she took off running. "Ruby, come back here! There's nothing down there."

"You're lying!" Ruby could hear the rising panic in his voice as she got closer to the prisoner at the end of the row. Footsteps pounded after her, but she didn't risk looking back. She would only have a few moments with the prisoner, but she had a feeling it would be enough, that whoever it was would answer the questions she had.

She skidded to a halt in front of the very last cell. In it was a man chained to the ground by both his hands and feet. He wore simple clothes just like the rest of the prisoners, and he was just sitting on the floor of his cell, even though he had room to go to his cot. When he heard Ruby, he looked up, and Ruby nearly fell backwards at the bright glow of his eyes. They were an ethereal purple, and a picture flashed into Ruby's mind as the guard that had chased her dragged her away.

She saw that man on top of a dragon.

"Thanks for trying," the older man said from behind the bars in his cell, snapping Ruby back to reality. The man in the purple robe shot him a glare, and the older man glared right back.

"You sure like trouble, don't you?" The man in purple sighed and seemed to be disappointed with her.

Ruby barely heard a word he said. She was too focused on grasping the picture in her mind, on trying to find something else from it.

"I don't know what that magic did to you, but it was the same dose as the first time." The man tapped a finger to his chin and thought while he stared right at Ruby. Then, his eyes seemed to brighten, and he clasped his hands together. "Ah, I understand! Your mental strength grew this last time around. Your resolve has been building. An unfortunate side effect of watching Dirk almost die, I suppose."

"Dirk," Ruby said, and suddenly, everything came back to her. Memories of Woodruff, of the dragon in the mountain, of the dwarves…all of it flooded into her mind. She remembered Dirk's body sprawled on the ground and how Woodruff had led her to a wonderful room so that she could rest. "You lied to me! Your promises were all false!"

"I understand it now! All of this is because you built such a strong mental connection with Dirk that he became your anchor! Now, I just need to figure out how to fix that, because you do need him to do your quests again. I will be back." Woodruff turned to the guards. "You two better watch her. Don't let her escape under any circumstance, or I personally will see to it that you both lose your heads."

Ruby threw herself onto her cot, her recent memories sluggishly returning to her. She still couldn't remember anything from before she'd woken up in the dungeon, and she wondered how many times she'd done this. All of it made her so angry, but there was nothing she could do. Hopelessness crawled over her skin, and she sank against the wall.

The only thing that she had learned was from the man with ethereal purple eyes. He'd brought that one single picture back to her of a dragon, but nothing more. She needed to see him again, but it was no use screaming like a child to be released. The only answers she could get were from Woodruff, so she waited for his return.

He didn't take long. There was a skip in his step when he approached her cell, and her eyes narrowed as she saw the same cup that she'd drank from before.

"Now, you don't want to die of thirst, do you?" Woodruff

said as he held the chalice out towards her. "Dirk certainly wouldn't want that." In the purple liquid, Dirk was all she could see.

"What is this?" Ruby asked. She wanted to look away, but she couldn't. She was watching everything she knew about Dirk play out in the liquid, from when they'd first met in the dungeon to when she'd raced him back to the kingdom on Sailor. Hesitantly, she took a swig of the liquid and then set it aside.

"The chalice is the true magic component," Woodruff explained, watching with excitement. "It's quite fascinating, really. It has a scent that changes based on the person, and it brings certain memory-tied emotions out of your mind. The problem is that without further modification, it works on all emotions equally. However, since you had such strong feelings for Dirk after you returned to the kingdom, which likely stemmed from his little fall, the chalice could not take in the full extent of those particular emotions, so your memories of Dirk were stronger. Now, though, as you think about Dirk, I've enchanted the chalice to pull those memories specifically from your mind. To balance it, you may feel hatred for Dirk."

"You can't do this!" Ruby tried to look away again, but she could feel herself forgetting her love for Dirk. She was beginning to forget him, and all that was left was hatred buried deep in her mind for someone she couldn't remember. She began to feel drowsy and laid down on her cot as her strength was sapped.

Woodruff waved a hand at her with a smile and turned to walk away, whistling a merry tune as he left.

POWERFUL

When Ruby opened her eyes, she didn't even remember falling asleep.

"Have your memories returned?"

She practically leaped out of her cot at the sound of someone else's voice. She saw the man in the purple robe standing in front of her cell.

"No," she said, her eyebrows furrowed.

"Do you remember what your quest is?" he asked, looking at her curiously. She felt like an experiment.

"Why wouldn't I?"

"Oh, concussions can be funny things. I'm just trying to make sure that you aren't forgetting new information, so tell me what you remember."

"You came to visit me earlier," she thought for a moment. "You said I have to fight a half-orc. Is it time already?" Ruby's eyes widened.

"No, child. You still have another hour to rest."

"If that's true, why are you interrupting me?"

The man laughed loudly. "There's your spark. I'll leave you to it," he said as he left with his two guards.

Ruby tried to silence the clamoring thoughts in her mind, but she couldn't. The challenge she had to face loomed in front of her like a death sentence. How was she possibly going to defeat something as formidable as a half-orc? Logically, she knew some of them were more human than orc, but she guessed the one that she was facing was more orc than human.

No, it wasn't a guess. Ruby could feel it in her bones. She didn't know why she was so certain, and it confused her, but there was nothing she could do except wait to see if she was right or not.

She had barely slept at all by the time the man returned, and she shook her head to rid herself of the drowsiness.

"How do you feel?" he asked her curiously, and she wondered if he truly did care. But she knew he didn't. If he did, he would do something to make it better, perhaps free her from her cell, but he would do nothing of the sort.

"Like not fighting an orc," Ruby groaned, turning over on her side. She wanted to sleep. "Can it be postponed? I'm not ready, and I'd like a chance to survive."

"Half-orc!" the man sounded triumphant. "No, your fight cannot be postponed. This kingdom doesn't exactly cater to its prisoners. I hope you understand."

"I don't understand, actually."

"As for that last part," he continued as if she hadn't spoken, "I have a feeling you'll do just fine out there."

"Was I a fighter before I was thrown in here for assassinating whoever it was?"

"Oh, yes. You were so good, in fact, that you were praised by witnesses for your impressive agility and skill. The way you snuck around the palace was incredible, and you would be a dangerous criminal to have out on the streets. Unless, of course, you willingly decide to put that skill to good use."

"What, like fighting an orc?" Ruby purposely didn't refer

to the beast as a half-orc—she knew he would correct her every single time.

"Precisely," the man beamed, "and it's a half-orc!"

"No." Ruby sat up and turned to face the man. "I think you want me for something else, for something bigger than fighting an orc. I think you need me to do something that no one else has done before, so I wonder, would you really let me die out there in that arena?" Ruby stared into the man's wide eyes.

He paled and quickly walked away from Ruby's cell towards his two henchmen. After a few whispered sentences to the guards, he went up the stairs without saying a word to Ruby.

"What," Ruby said to the henchmen, "am I right?"

They ignored her.

In truth, Ruby wanted to survive, but it was hard to be motivated when she didn't have anything to survive for. Her memories were gone, and there was a hatred buried inside of her for living without them. When she really thought about it, the only emotion she felt was hatred: hatred for this cell, hatred for the pompous man, hatred for being forced to survive…every breath she took was coated with it. The only triumph she felt was getting the best of people, and if the only way to do that was by not fighting the half-orc, then she would do so. That way, either she would die and not have to worry, or she would live without having to try.

The man returned moments later, cradling a familiar golden chalice between his hands.

"This will help your memories return," he offered her a strained smile, "but only if you really focus. Try to remember before you lost them. Think hard, and if you see pictures, that means it's working."

Ruby knew he was lying. The deceit was written all over his face, but she stared into the chalice anyway. What was there to lose? Besides, once she looked, she found it impossible to turn her head.

"I see nothing," Ruby said, though she was starting to feel drained.

The man pulled it away. "You're telling the truth," he said in wonder.

"Why would I lie?"

The man ignored her and went to his henchmen. He whispered to them some more and left the chalice on the floor outside of Ruby's cell.

"You're acting strange," he said.

"Maybe it's because I don't have my memories."

"No, it's something else." He studied her for another moment before continuing. "If you choose not to fight today, I assure you that death will follow. No one is going to save you."

"You're bluffing."

"Are you willing to risk your life to find out?"

"Yes."

The man stared her down, his eyebrows pinched in the middle of his forehead.

"Well," he sighed, "this should be a very interesting battle to watch, shouldn't it?"

He unlocked Ruby's cell and guided her up the stairs. His henchmen followed behind her, and she hated the way their eyes bored into her back.

She found herself walking down a hallway that curved as though the whole thing was a circle.

"Palaces are so unnecessarily gaudy," Ruby commented.

"You're very ungrateful," the man said.

"There's isn't much for me to be grateful for."

"For starters, you should be grateful that you're setting foot inside a hallway that very few people even get to see."

"Why would I care about fancy floors?" Ruby asked when

the man stopped walking. "Do tell me, because I would very much like to know your answer."

The man merely shrugged and opened the door in front of him. Ruby was ushered in, and she found herself in a room full of dangerous-looking weapons. "What will it be?"

Ruby walked around the room slowly, looking over each of the options. She ran a finger down the blade of a sword and looked right at one of the henchmen. He stared right back at her fearlessly, and something in her wanted to give him something to be afraid of.

Without thinking, she grabbed a pair of obsidian daggers that sat next to the sword and heaved one of them at the wall, smirking as the blade sliced through the air and sunk deep into the wall next to the guard's head.

To his credit, all she had seen was a slight flinch.

"Impressive," Ruby commented while the man dressed in purple stormed over to her.

"What were you thinking?" he screamed, securing her hands in a vice-like grip so she couldn't do any more damage.

Ruby smirked. "See? You care what I do, because I bet you aren't going to let him kill me."

She jerked her chin at the furious guard, who had walked toward her with fury in his eyes. Ruby pushed the noble to the side, ready to face the henchman, but she'd been right.

"Stop!" the man in purple screamed. "Do not harm a hair on her head!"

The henchman obeyed, and Ruby walked up to the man in purple, whose face was completely red.

"Told you." She tapped a finger to her chin the way the man always did. "Now, I'm willing to bet that your next move would be to cuff my hands, or send me into the arena without a weapon, or both, but if you do, you only lower my chances of winning, and I know you want me to survive, so I think you're still going to give me a weapon."

The man reluctantly nodded and backed away, but Ruby certainly didn't miss the angry lines in his face. He was furious with her, and it was inexplicably thrilling.

Again, Ruby took her time to walk around the room and check out the various weapons. In the end, she picked an intricately designed spear that was probably the weakest weapon in the room.

"Interesting," the man murmured. If he had a notepad, Ruby had a feeling he would have been taking notes right then.

"What is?" Ruby asked. "That I picked a weapon that definitely won't help me survive against an orc?"

The man didn't even bother to correct her. "No, not that. As for whether you'll survive or not, I know you will. You're going to fight because that's what you do—that's who you are. A survivor."

"I would ask how you know, but I don't suppose you'd tell me," Ruby remarked.

"Correct."

"Well, I'd tell you that you don't know me at all. That much, I'll say. But I know it'll do you no good, so I'll just prove it in the arena." She stood at the edge of the room when a trap door opened. Instead of falling, as she'd guessed the man had intended for her to do, she simply jumped down. "Wish me luck," she called, flashing a sardonic smile up at the scowling noble.

The men who were working the trap doors on the floor of the arena climbed the ladder up to the room with the weapons and closed the doors behind them. Ruby turned away from the wall and as the crowd cheered, a giant creature that looked almost human but with green skin and much larger features faced her. Spittle flew out of his mouth when he let out a deafening roar.

Ruby just laughed. "You sure are hideous, aren't you?" she yelled, and he turned his anger on her. Above them somewhere, an announcer was speaking, though Ruby could barely hear him.

She charged at the half-orc and only barely moved herself out of the way of his axe. Every time the half-orc missed, it was just barely, and she hoped that the man in purple was watching.

During one of the last blows from the half-orc's axe that she ducked, she turned to see that there were guards at the edge of the arena watching her every move. That was when she knew she was right. The noble needed her alive for something bigger than a lowly arena fight.

Ruby ran toward the guards and stopped a few paces in front of them, waiting as the half-orc's measured stomps rumbled through the ground.

"Fight!" one of the guards yelled, only confirming Ruby's suspicions.

She turned her back to the half-orc as he charged at her, and she carelessly dropped her weapon on the floor of the arena.

"No."

The guards couldn't hide the panic on their faces, their stunned expressions were obvious, even under their helmets. Ruby watched them with a smirk while the half-orc's shadow loomed over her.

She did want to fight. Surprisingly enough, the man in purple had been right about that much, but Ruby wouldn't give him the satisfaction. She told herself that fighting to live or fighting for what she didn't have was useless. Somewhere deep inside her, Ruby figured that if she kept playing by the noble's rules, she would never get her answers. It just seemed like the way of the kingdom. She didn't know if it was a gut feeling or a memory from before, but it was there, and she trusted it. If she truly didn't have a reason to keep fighting, she wouldn't bother.

"Stop!" the man in purple yelled over the murmuring crowd. As soon as the guards heard him, they launched their spears at the half-orc. When the half-orc's weapon thudded into the ground next to her, she realized just how close she had been to dying. She walked toward the dying beast and jumped up onto his stomach as he collapsed onto his back.

"Why did you kill those people?" she asked as the creature died. It swatted at her with its hands, but it was too weak to even lift them off the ground. "Tell me."

"Slaves," the half-orc gasped. "I was a slave. My whole family was. I wanted them to be free, so I killed him."

He struggled up to one of his elbows. "Why didn't you kill me?"

"Just wanted to try something," Ruby said, "and it appears that I was right to suspect that this kingdom needs me alive."

"How fortunate," the half-orc snorted derisively, falling heavily onto his back. "These are the worst kinds of people. Don't ever side with them." The beast's lips twisted into a satisfied smile, and he coughed weakly. "I think you made them mad."

Those were his last words as he closed his eyes and died on the arena dirt. Both of the spears the guards had thrown were lodged deep into the half-orc's stomach, and the men approached to collect them.

Ruby straightened and looked down at the half-orc. She could respect his effort to fight, both for his family and against Ruby, even if it was all in vain. There was some familiarity there that Ruby couldn't quite place, but she understood that his death had a purpose.

Suddenly, she was shoved into the dirt.

"Who do you think you are?" the man in purple bellowed from behind her. "You'll be thrown in the arena again, and again, and again, until you fight back! You'll do as expected of you, or you'll never get your answers!"

"You wouldn't have given them to me even if I had fought!" From the ground, Ruby spit on the noble's shoe.

His face purpled in anger, and he seized Ruby's collar, hauling her to her feet. "You know nothing!"

"Are you sure about that?"

The man threw her back again, but she stayed on her feet this time. They were out of sight from most of the crowd, save for the onlookers directly across, and Ruby could feel them watching the spectacle with interest.

"You will never disrespect me like that again! You can rot in the dungeon for all I care!"

"Oh, but you do care," Ruby snarled, jabbing a finger into his chest. "If you didn't, you would have let me die out there." Ruby shrugged. "Such a pity. I guess it's your fault for embarrassing yourself like that. I told you I wouldn't fight, and you didn't believe me, so that's on you."

"Stop this." A new voice entered the conversation, and the man in purple stood ramrod straight. He moved out of Ruby's way, and she saw a man that couldn't have been anything but the ruler of the kingdom.

The king was dressed in an ornate blue and white suit with intricate gold patterns on it to match his impressively long cape. It draped over his shoulders and flowed behind him to drag on the filthy arena floor. "You've made me ruin this cape for you, Woodruff."

"Your Majesty," he said, bowing. He elbowed Ruby hard in the leg to do so as well, and Ruby almost laughed. Did he truly expect her to bow?

Instead, Ruby marched right up to the king. A golden crown sat on his head, and the jewels that decorated it glinted with every movement the king made. Immediately, the guards that flanked him stepped forward, so she stopped right in front of them and stared directly at the king.

"My memories," she demanded, as though he could just hand them to her right there.

"You will get them back." The king waved a hand at the guards, and they stepped back. There was a fearlessness in his bright eyes that matched Ruby's own. "I will not play games with you as, I'm afraid, Woodruff has. I will tell you outright that I did take your memories, and it was for a reason you do not yet understand. If you succeed in this next quest, though, I assure you that you will never have to see Woodruff again, and I personally will see to it that your memories are returned."

"You admitted to taking them. Why should I trust you to give them back?"

"Because I am the only one who can. I understand your reason for distrust, and I admit, you have completed quests for me before, but I need you to do just one more for me. This one is different. This one will help you, I think."

Ruby stared at him skeptically, and he sighed. "Woodruff, run along now—I must talk to our prisoner in private."

Woodruff's expression soured. He lingered a bit, as if he wanted to say something further.

"Leave, Woodruff," the king commanded more forcefully. Woodruff obeyed immediately. Ruby didn't have time to wonder what that had been about before the king turned to her.

"I am curious to see what you'll say to convince me," she frowned, crossing her arms.

"It is not what I will say, but who you will meet," the king said. "His name is Dirk. He will come by your cell before the quest, and he will be with you during it. You will understand."

Ruby just rolled her eyes, though the name only brought her feelings of happiness. "We'll see about that," she said.

"You will accept my quest once you meet him. I am sure of it."

"Very well." Ruby just wanted to get out of there.

The king dipped his head. "Good. Woodruff will prepare you, as will Dirk. I will see you off when you leave."

His guards followed him as he turned and walked away, though one lingered behind. He looked at Ruby and whispered six simple words, but they nearly brought her to her knees.

"The man with the purple eyes."

At first, Ruby didn't understand, but when she thought about the words, she remembered running down the length of the dungeon, sprinting towards a cell that held the very man the guard had described. He'd been on the floor, hands and feet chained, and the image of the man on top of the dragon was burned into her mind.

"Why are you helping me?" Ruby whispered as the guard started to walk away.

"There are things the king does not know about Woodruff. I believe you can help him get away from that crooked man."

Ruby had a thousand more questions, but the guard had hurried back to the king's side. She watched them leave, still reeling from the new information.

ONLY HATRED

*R*uby spent a lot of the time in her cell glancing down towards the far end of the dungeon. She could practically sense the mysterious man's presence—she couldn't stop wondering if it was because he was powerful, or because knowing he was there played tricks on her mind.

She thought she heard him move. It was a soft sound, one that would have blended into the background if she wasn't listening hard enough, but she heard the echo of his chains and felt sorry for him. She wondered what her connection to him was, why he was so powerful, and what he had done to be locked up not only in a cell, but in chains as well.

Footsteps sounded, and Woodruff approached Ruby's cell. She wondered how he would behave, now that the king wasn't there to bring him to heel.

"And thus, your next mission begins," he started dramatically. Ruby could tell he was trying to project confidence, as if Ruby's spectacle in the arena hadn't affected him at all. "It's a new location that I don't believe you've been to. You and your squire will sail for an island off the coast tomorrow morning."

"A squire?" Ruby asked, watching his face carefully.

"Yes, and I suggest not killing him, though you seem to be rather good at that," Woodruff commented.

Ruby just laughed. "First, it angers you when I do not kill someone, and now you'd be angry if I did. How fascinating," she chuckled, a mocking smile on her lips.

He just rolled his eyes. "I'll let him deal with you. Maybe he'll survive this time."

Ruby sighed internally. Now that she knew that the king did, in fact, have her memories, she couldn't care less about Woodruff's verbal jabs.

He left before she could say anything, and a shockingly familiar man stepped into the dim lighting of the dungeon. He avoided Ruby's eyes, but she knew she'd worked with him before, not only because Woodruff had implied it, but because he was recognizable. There was warmth around him, and she felt an unexpected pull of affection. Regardless of what had happened before, those were the two things that she associated with him.

"I've worked with you before," Ruby said, and the man nodded.

"Dirk," he responded, offering his hand through the bars. Ruby took it. Suddenly, she understood that the king was right, that she would be more willing to do this quest once she met Dirk.

"Look at me," she said softly, and he did, and both of them were stricken at the sight of each other's faces. There was a world of warmth in his eyes, and Ruby knew he was, perhaps, the one thing in existence that she couldn't hate.

"You must get fitted for your armor," Dirk said suddenly, snapping out of whatever spell the two had been under. Ruby just nodded and backed away while he opened the door. Woodruff had left a chest, and Dirk flipped the lid over to reveal the shiny metal piled inside. "Do you want help?"

"Yes, please," Ruby said, and Dirk just looked at her with a tiny hint of a smile. Ruby stared back blankly.

Whatever had occurred between them, she couldn't let that affect this quest. She let Dirk help her suit up, though it felt strange to not speak to him. The silence in her cell was heavy.

"Who is the man at the end of the dungeon?" she asked quietly. Somehow, she had the feeling she could trust Dirk with her life.

"I don't know," Dirk replied. "He's been here for a long time, but I have no idea why."

Ruby knew he was lying—he knew something about the man. Hurt spread through her heart. What if she was wrong to trust him?

"Don't tell anyone I asked you about him, please," Ruby pleaded once he had finished with the armor. Dirk just nodded absentmindedly as he looked over the straps that held it together. "Dirk, I'm serious."

"I won't." He looked up at her. Ruby knew he wasn't lying.

She looked down at her armor, at the designs carved into it. "This is beautiful."

Dirk smiled. "Try not to die inconveniently." When Ruby stared blankly, his face changed to a serious one, and he avoided her eyes.

"What do you mean?" Ruby tried.

"It's just a joke," Dirk sighed. "Squires are meant to be the ones who come back if the adventurer doesn't. If you die, I'm supposed to retrieve the armor and bring it back."

Ruby ran her finger along one of the edges. It looked warped, like it had been melted. "Was I wearing this when it happened?"

Dirk just stared at what she was referring to. Ruby was about to give up on getting answers from him when he gave a reluctant nod.

Ruby smiled.

Dirk started taking her armor off for her, and Ruby realized how comfortable it had felt, how right. It was big and chunky and heavy, but she knew she had definitely worn that very piece before.

Once Dirk had all the armor back in the chest, he left in a hurry without saying anything. Ruby sat down at her cot and looked towards the end of the dungeon again.

Later in the day, footsteps sounded outside of the prison door. Ruby only realized she'd been hoping it was Dirk and was disappointed when Woodruff appeared.

"Dirk said your armor fit wonderfully!" Woodruff was back to his cheerful self, but Ruby wanted to skip whatever his false pleasantries were.

"That orc said he was a slave to the family he had killed," Ruby said, slinking up to the nobleman.

"Half-orc," Woodruff corrected pointedly. "They lie. They are very good at it, actually. Every creature has their quirks. That half-orc was just trying to turn you against the king with his dying breath. How unfortunate for him that he wasted it on you."

Ruby laughed. "That might be the first funny thing you've said. Ironic, too, that you seem to waste all your breath by talking to me when all I do is make trouble for you."

Woodruff narrowed his eyes. "You are right, Ruby—you have been a struggle to deal with, but what fun is anything if it isn't a challenge?" Woodruff pulled an arm around from behind his back. In it sat a beautiful headdress. "Here's yours."

"More armor to make sure I return alive? How kind of you."

"Precisely." Woodruff opened the prison cell door and placed it on Ruby's head. Immediately, a dull ache appeared. Ruby tried to pull it off, but she couldn't. "If you do not return to the kingdom alive with the dragon scales, you die. Do you understand?"

Ruby wanted to punch Woodruff, and from the satisfied grin on his face, she knew that he could tell.

"As soon as I'm free of all of this, I'm going to kill you," Ruby said matter-of-factly.

"Oh, no. You will never be allowed to return back to this kingdom. If you do, regardless of whether you succeed or not, I guarantee that you'll end up right back here—without your memories and being sent to die."

The last three words Woodruff said sent a jolt through Ruby's bones, like a memory buried deep within her trying to come to the surface. Woodruff had sent someone to die before, and they had—that was all she could remember, but not who, not what, and not why.

"I'll leave you to prepare yourself mentally," Woodruff said, locking Ruby up again. "You'll be sailing to an island with Dirk—rumors of a dragon and islanders that worship it have been brought to my attention. You are to return with three dragon scales. If you don't..." Woodruff dragged a finger across his neck and started to walk away, but then, he stopped. "Oh! And I suggest, if you see me again before you leave, you should be a little nicer to me. After all, I can make this quest so much more difficult for you. All it'll take is a couple wrong words from you, and ha! No weapons, no squire, and perhaps you could swim to the island instead. I can take anything from you, and if the need arises, that's exactly what I'll do."

Ruby vibrated with fury as she watched him leave. She tried to burn it off by pacing around her cell, but it did nothing to calm her rage. At the very least, she was full of energy and ready to face the dragon on the island.

Dirk had returned while she still pacing and muttering to herself.

"Something on your mind?" he asked curiously.

"Woodruff," Ruby growled.

"Don't let him get under your skin—he's all bark, no bite, just like most nobles are."

"But he's infuriating!" Ruby turned on Dirk. She didn't have the capacity to feel any warmth towards him at the moment. "How do you stand him?"

Dirk shrugged and started to take a step back, but stopped. "You get used to him. I didn't know he would anger you so much."

"Well, he does. Can we get going now?"

Dirk dipped his head and opened the cell door. Ruby walked past him, even though she had no idea where she was going. Dirk caught up and led the way.

"You really don't remember anything from before?" Dirk asked.

"No. Let's just get this quest over with."

Dirk opened his mouth as if he wanted to say something, but he didn't. They walked down the hallway but went past the armor room until they got to a straight corridor. Ruby could hear voices through the walls.

"This is the main part of the palace," Dirk said.

"Why are you telling me?"

"I don't know, I just…I was just trying to make conversation."

"How about you make conversation by telling me who I am?" Ruby stopped in her tracks and looked right at Dirk. "Do you know how lost I feel, to know nothing of anything before this kingdom? I've been a pawn here before—the king himself told me—and it sucks!"

"You spoke to the king?"

"That's not the point!" Ruby hissed. She wanted to trust Dirk. She wanted him to be the reason she wasn't so angry all the time, but if he was lying to her and refusing to tell her anything, he wasn't someone she would trust. "Tell me, Dirk."

"I can't do that," he said quietly, and he continued walking. Ruby stayed where she was. Eventually, Dirk turned around. "If you don't come, I'll have to call the guards, Ruby."

"Fine. Call them, then." Ruby crossed her arms. "Walking with you willingly is worse."

"Ruby—"

"I'm not moving." Ruby held true to her word and stood there. She wanted to believe that Dirk wouldn't call the guards, but she would have been wrong to do so.

"Guards!" Dirk yelled, though there was regret in his eyes as he stared right at Ruby. She looked down at the ground. Now, it seemed, there really was only hatred left inside of her.

Two guards came running down the hallway. They stopped when they saw Dirk. "The prisoner is not cooperating," he told them, nodding at Ruby.

Both of the guards marched towards Ruby and grabbed an arm each. Ruby didn't bother fighting them—she let them pull her along down the hallway. Dirk followed behind them quietly.

Ruby wanted to scream at him, but she knew her silence would bother him more, so she stayed quiet as she was pulled through a side door and thrown onto the ground in a patch of grass. Dirk rushed to her side to help her up, but Ruby didn't let him.

"Come on," he pleaded, "trust me."

"On what grounds?" Ruby spat, shoving his offered hand aside and standing on her own.

"Lover's quarrel?"

Ruby turned and saw Woodruff standing in front of her, but her attention was pulled more to what the front of the palace looked like.

Flourishing gardens stretched out on either side of them to curl gracefully around the palace. In front of her, though, waves rippled against the sand that came up to the gardens. It was a beautiful sight, and Ruby almost wished this was where her home was. How could something so stunning be full of such horrible people?

"Quiet, Woodruff." Dirk walked around Ruby and strode down towards the sands. Ruby could see ships farther down the coast, where wooden docks stretched out into the sea.

"Very well. I won't tell you about your crew, nor will I tell you which ship is yours."

Ruby didn't care what Woodruff had threatened her with, anger simmered hotly under her skin. She marched up to him and seized the collar of his shirt, pulling him towards her.

"Which ship?" she hissed, throwing him back the same way the guards had thrown her. They rushed up to her and wrenched her arms behind her back.

"Let her go!" Woodruff snapped. He'd stayed on his feet, but only barely.

"You just prove again and again, Woodruff, that you don't want me harmed," Ruby said as the guards unhanded her.

Woodruff laughed. "You're a conceited one, aren't you? I'm surprised you aren't a royal."

"Take us to the ship, Woodruff," Dirk said. Ruby wanted to slap the smug smirk off Woodruff's face, but Dirk stood in between them and kept them an arm's length away from each other.

"Enough!" he yelled, genuinely angry. He turned to Ruby. "Do you want your freedom? Do you want to be done with this?"

Ruby backed down.

Woodruff did the same, and they walked on either side of Dirk. Ruby felt like a squabbling child when Dirk had stepped in. Honestly, she just wanted to make Woodruff hurt, and she very well could have, if it was just the two of them. She was much stronger than he was, and that was a fight she would be determined to win.

Seagulls cawed overhead, flying in circles over the group. The sound of the waves brought peace to Ruby, and she tried to let her anger dissipate, but she couldn't. Still, she took measured breaths of the sea air to quell her irritation.

They approached the docks, and they swayed as they stepped onto the old wood. Ruby stumbled as it swayed, but shouldered past Dirk when he stopped to help her.

"This is your ship," Woodruff said, stopping in front of a vessel that was significantly smaller than the others. Still, it looked like a powerful little thing, with the same color scheme of white and light blue as the palace.

She climbed up the stairs that were rigged by rope to the side of the ship and walked through the gangway. A crew was working tirelessly with the sails, and Ruby was greeted by a man who she could only assume was the captain.

"Captain Devereux, at your service," he announced, offering a hand to Ruby. He looked cunning—his braided hair was tied up in a bun on the back of his head, and his eyes were bluer than the sea. A wide smile spread across his face, and instantly, Ruby had a vague sense of distrust.

"He truly is the best," Woodruff said, stepping around Ruby to stand next to the captain.

Captain Devereux laughed in response, and that was when Ruby truly knew she couldn't trust him. "We sailed all the time when we were younger! This scoundrel grew up in the palace but ran away to sail the seas. Only came back when his ship was blown to bits by an armada of dwarves. He washed up on a plank of wood, begging for a new ship."

"I work for him now," Devereux said, patting Woodruff on the back before greeting Dirk. The squire looked queasy already. "A well-paying job, and I still don't have to be stuck at the palace. Besides, with Renegade here," he said, tapping the side of the ship, "we really taught those dwarves a lesson."

"I told you, her name cannot be Renegade if you're working for the king!" Woodruff exclaimed with mock exasperation.

"I can't just change her name." Devereux seemed serious enough about that to make Woodruff back off from the subject.

"Well, I wish you all luck. Your armor, portions of food and water, and weapons are all on board, though Devereux is free to take them from you if you act up," Woodruff said, looking right at Ruby. Her attention was pulled away before she could respond—the king was approaching with what looked to be a small army of guards to see them off, just as he had promised.

"Woodruff!" the king called, clear warning in his voice. "Leave them be!"

"Better get off the ship," Ruby said, stepping towards Woodruff. She didn't care if the captain was watching her threaten Woodruff. "Your master wants you back." Woodruff wanted to say something, but he seemed to know the king wouldn't be pleased.

"Maybe you'll die," he said flippantly, sending her a smarmy smile over his shoulder, "and then you'd finally be out of my hair."

"Woodruff?" Ruby called, casually leaning against the side of the ship, "How does it feel to be trapped in the palace all day long? I think it's been driving you a little bit insane, and that is definitely not a good look on you. It makes you quite easy to provoke when you're careless."

Woodruff paused on his way down. His hands clenched into trembling fists, but he kept himself pulled together and continued his descent. A few members of the crew approached to pull up the steps.

Devereux turned to Ruby, surprise in his piercing blue eyes. "Aren't you the little rebel," he remarked.

"I'm not a rebel," Ruby turned to look at him. "I just don't have anyone to fight for but myself."

Devereux simply nodded and returned to the wheel. Ruby stayed at the side of the ship, and the king locked eyes with her as the ship began to pull away from the dock. She could practically hear the king's voice telling her that he was right, that this quest was one she wanted to complete.

She'd believed him, but now, she was starting to have her doubts. For a time now she'd felt an inner voice shouting at her to be suspicious. Though she felt paranoid at the thought, there was some part of her that felt as if she'd been forced into serving the king for a long time already…

Her thoughts were broken by the footsteps of Dirk on the creaking deck of the Renegade. She studiously ignored him. All his presence was doing was making her angry. She wanted to shove him overboard, but she didn't want to risk getting killed—not yet. Not until she knew for certain whether fighting for herself was worth it or not.

WHENEVER THE WATER STIRS

*R*enegade smoothly sailed over the waves of the ocean. Ruby had been given a room belowdecks, but she spent most of her time leaning over the railing, feeling the breeze on her skin and in her hair. She savored the feeling, it was something she hadn't even known existed.

She wondered if she did this earlier in her life, if she spent a lot of time sailing before she was taken by this kingdom. Considering that the kingdom was practically right on the water, she wouldn't have been surprised if she had. She hoped she did, because the feeling was wonderful.

"We'll be at the islands in two days' time."

Ruby turned to see that one of the female crew members had come up beside her to stare out into the ocean.

"Incredible, isn't it?"

"Do you ever get tired of it?" Ruby asked. This was the first girl she'd gotten to speak to since her memories had been taken, and she liked her already.

"No!" she said with confidence. "Never. I mean, sure, it looks the same. There are always waves, sometimes they're higher or lower, and there's always water and sky and sun, but don't you smell it?" She closed her eyes, and Ruby copied her, but all there was in the air was the tang of salt.

"Smell what?" Ruby asked, her eyes still closed.

"Land." The girl paused and took a deep breath. "It's strange, I know, but you can always sense your destination. It's there, dancing on the wind—the smell of cherries on the island chain we're going to, or the stronger smell of salt to the east, where many of the monsters live in the deeper waters, or to the west, the sweeter smell of the western kingdoms."

Ruby opened her eyes. "I can't smell any of that."

Maybe that meant she wasn't a sailor before her memories were taken.

"That's what everyone says," the girl grinned widely. "Maybe I just have a gift. My name is Melody."

"I'm Ruby," she responded. "What do you do on the ship?"

"Mostly, we sing and drink. When we're working, though, I'm the captain's first mate. I do all of the tasks he's too busy to do, like get word around to the crew if there's a change in course or decide who does what for the trip."

"That sounds incredible," Ruby mused, and she meant it.

"I've got a good feeling about you, Ruby. There's always a place for you if you want to stay. I've got to get to work, though."

Melody cheerily waved over her shoulder and walked off towards Devereux, who was holding a steady course straight towards the open water.

Ruby closed her eyes and tried to smell the cherries, and maybe it was her imagination, but she caught a whiff of the tangy fruit. She smiled and opened her eyes again.

She would have liked to stay. It was a tempting thought, to abandon this quest and live out her short days until the headdress killed her on the sea. Woodruff would hate her, and that's what made the thought all the more enticing.

Still, she needed to see if she really would get the answers the king promised. This quest was supposed to be good for her, and she intended to find out if that was true or not. Perhaps she would return to Renegade and join the crew once everything was over.

Two days had passed since they'd left, and the sun had started to dip low in the sky. According to Melody, they would arrive at the islands tomorrow morning. Ruby left the railings for her room and laid down in a bed much more comfortable than the cot she'd been given in her prison cell.

The space was cozy. There was a desk and a wardrobe, both of which were attached to the metal inside of the ship. Two slots above Ruby's head marked other beds that, at the push of a button, could be rolled out and secured by a couple of metal bars. A door in the center of one of the walls led to Dirk's room, and in between them, they shared a bathroom.

Ruby stayed awake for a while, watching the sun sink lower and lower out of her little window. Thoughts of Dirk intruded on the calming night, and Ruby opened her window in an attempt to focus on the sound of the ocean, but Dirk was still in her head.

Ruby tossed one of her many pillows at the wall. All she wanted was a straight answer, and she'd thought Dirk was with her to help her. He seemed to like her a lot, but she couldn't understand how he expected her to even tolerate him when all he did was hide things from her and lie to her.

Even when the sun was far below the water, Ruby was wide awake. She bundled herself up in her blanket as the night got colder, and though the warmth of it should have helped coax her to sleep, it didn't.

She slipped on a pair of heavy cotton pants and a similar long-sleeved shirt that Devereux had provided her when he realized she'd brought no clothes other than the simple ones on her body. They were too big for her, and they were probably from Devereux himself, but they were cozy. They protected her from the cold as she stepped out into the corridor and then onto the deck.

She gasped when she looked up. It was full of stars, and Ruby knew she had seen them before, but she didn't realize there were so many. They flickered against the dark sky, and Ruby couldn't tear her eyes away.

"You like the stars?" Ruby turned to see Devereux still at the wheel. He was the one who had called out to her, though Melody was standing next to him. They seemed to be in the middle of a conversation.

"Yes." Ruby didn't trust him, but she didn't mind talking to him, especially if Melody was there too.

"Why are you awake?" Ruby asked her.

Melody shrugged. Her green eyes were as bright as the stars above, and in the light of the moon, she looked ethereal as the wind played with the ends of her hair. "I can never sleep the night before we dock. I don't know why."

"Can you take over for a moment?" Devereux asked Melody. "I want to show the girl something."

"My name is Ruby."

"Ruby, my apologies." Devereux walked away from the wheel and towards the stern of the ship. He looked down at the water, and Ruby followed his gaze.

Much like the sky above, the water was twinkling. Little green lights leaped in the spray as the ship moved through the water.

"What are they?" she asked in amazement.

"Bioluminescent creatures," Devereux said, and he sounded just as fascinated as she was. "I don't know why they do that, but whenever the water stirs, they follow it. Incredible little things, they are."

Ruby nodded. "How simple a life they have," she said.

He chuckled. "Are you jealous?"

"At least they have a clear purpose in their lives," Ruby said coldly. "I don't have my memories. The man I'm supposed to trust won't tell me anything, and I've done a quest like this before for the king—I just can't remember it." Ruby paused. She didn't know why she was telling Devereux all of this, but she kept speaking. "I'm being used, and I can't do anything about it. I just want to be free."

"Hmm." Devereux studied her for a moment. "You can change your destiny. You're, what, Osmiri?"

Ruby blinked in astonishment. "Osmiri…" she repeated. It sounded somewhat familiar. "Why do you say that?"

"Oh, you travel to as many ports as I do and the little things start to add up. The way you hold yourself, the faint accent, a tan that's just a shade darker than most of those in Torbek." He paused. "You don't know where you're from?" he prodded hesitantly.

Ruby shook her head slowly.

"Mm. Then perhaps there is little keeping you here." Devereux scratched at the stubble on his chin. "Melody mentioned that she offered you a position on our crew. I stand by that offer too. We're always in need of another hand."

"You work for the king of Torbek."

"That's more of a pleasantry. Yes, he has me deliver goods from the islands or the western kingdoms sometimes, but when we're at sea, we do what we like. Most of the places we go are places we wanted to go, anyways, so the king doesn't truly have control over us."

"Well, he has direct control over me," Ruby laughed bitterly. "I have to do this quest."

"What does he have over you?"

Ruby just looked at Devereux and shook her head. "My life."

"Oh." Devereux finally looked up from the water.

"He promised that once I finished this quest, I'd get my memories back." Ruby sighed. "He promised, but there's nothing I can do if he doesn't follow through and keeps sending me out to run his stupid errands."

"Sometimes, all you can do is hope that a promise is true," Devereux sent her a sympathetic look.

"Yeah, well, it's not enough." Ruby turned to go back to her cabin, an unfamiliar ache in her chest. "Goodnight, Devereux."

"Good night, sailor."

Ruby stopped suddenly. That word was familiar.

"Have we met before?" She sent the captain a searching gaze. The man didn't seem familiar, but something had stirred inside her when he'd called her a sailor.

"No," Devereux said, standing up straight and turning to face Ruby.

"Are you lying to me?"

"I have no reason to."

Ruby practically leaped at him and pressed him against the edge of his own ship. His eyes were wide, and there was genuine shock on his face. "Maybe you're more under the king's thumb than I thought. Maybe this is some kind of trick so the king has an excuse to say I'm not loyal and lock me up again."

"I've done nothing of the sort!" Devereux growled. He suddenly pushed against Ruby and used the momentum to flip them over. Where Ruby had just grabbed the collar of his shirt with her hands, he pressed an arm to her neck, effectively choking her. "Do not ever pull a stunt like that again!" He backed away from her and collected himself while Ruby caught her breath. "Now, if you would like to have a civilized conversation, perhaps I can help you."

Ruby spat on the deck and walked away, brimming with anger. She was mostly mad at herself for telling Devereux everything and truly hoping he would be of some use, even though she'd felt as if she couldn't trust him the moment she stepped on his ship.

She stormed past Melody, who she still wanted to trust but couldn't, and walked right into Dirk.

"Woah," he said, stopping Ruby. "I heard yelling. What's going on?"

Ruby ignored him and returned to her room, slamming the door shut. She heard Dirk's footsteps outside her room, and he started pounding on her door.

"Come on, talk to me!"

"Only when you start telling me the truth!" Ruby yelled, putting a pillow over her ears. The knocking stopped, and she heard Dirk return to his room. When he opened the bathroom door on his side, though, Ruby understood what he was doing.

"Don't you dare," she said coldly, retrieving her spear from where it sat propped up against her desk. It was unfortunate that the bathroom doors could only be locked from the inside.

Dirk opened her door and stumbled back when he saw her hefting the spear. "Seriously, Ruby?"

"Yes, seriously!" she cried, stepping forward and driving Dirk backwards. "All anyone ever does is lie to me, and I'm tired of it. I won't work with you if you won't tell me everything you know about me."

"Ruby, I can't," Dirk pleaded, "but you'll learn everything once this quest is over, I promise. If you don't trust the king, then trust me."

"I trust the king far more than I trust you," Ruby growled. "He's the only one that's been even remotely honest with me. Now, leave!"

"No, I won't." Dirk moved forward and pushed Ruby's spear aside. She backed up, trying to put it in front of Dirk to keep him away from her, but he closed the distance in between them until he was right in front of her. "Listen, you can trust me, I promise, and I want to tell you, but I can't. I can't speak about any of it, okay?"

"Why not?" Ruby demanded, but it was hard to hold strong when he was this close to her.

"Just…trust me, please. I know you feel that you can—that's because you trusted me last time."

"Who am I, Dirk? What do you know about me?" Ruby asked again.

"No more than what you've guessed."

"That's not an answer!" Ruby threw her spear to the ground and shoved him away before crawling into her bed. She turned away from him. "Leave," she demanded again.

Dirk sighed. "I wish you'd talk to me."

"Yeah? Well, I wish I knew who I was."

"Give me a chance."

"Leave."

Finally, Dirk sighed in defeat and left through the bathroom door. He closed both Ruby's and his behind him as he returned to his room.

Tears rolled down Ruby's cheeks. She could still feel so much hatred inside of her that she felt like screaming, but there was also a deep desire to simply lean on someone who had all of the answers. She wanted to trust someone, anyone, so badly that she was sure that it was the source of her anger.

Moonlight shimmered through her window, and shadows danced across the corner of her room. She cried there silently, wondering how her life became all of this, and within moments, she fell into a tumultuous sleep.

A WILD GREEN ISLAND

*R*uby was roused by the shouts of the crew early in the morning. She looked out of her window and saw that they'd docked on a beautiful island full of lush, green plants.

The idea of having a chance to explore excited her, though the heavy emotions of the previous night still lingered in her chest. She was still upset by everything and wasn't in the mood to see anyone, but she figured that it would be better to simply move on, or at the very least, to pretend like she had.

So, she took off the clothes Devereux had given her and wore the simple ones she'd had as long as she could remember. When she walked outside, she could feel the crew's eyes on her, but she ignored all of them.

Dirk, Devereux, and Melody were standing on the gangway. When they saw Ruby, each had a different response— Dirk looked away, guilt all over his face. Devereux held her eyes as though he was challenging her to act the way she had last night. Melody was the one who walked up to her, pity and uncertainty warring in her gaze.

"Are you alright?" Melody asked, and Ruby didn't know how to answer her, so she didn't. She simply walked past her and off the ship, and if she were in a better mood, she would have stopped to admire the beauty of the island around her.

"Ruby, wait!" Dirk ran down the unsteady steps after her, managing to carry both her chest of armor and her spear. Ruby stopped and watched him chase after her. When he was in front of her, he paused to catch his breath and set down both of the things he'd been carrying. "You don't have to talk to me or hear me talk. Just let me come with you for this."

Again, Ruby chose not to answer. She both wanted him there and didn't want him there. The quest would be difficult without him, and she was afraid to be alone on an island she knew nothing about, but she didn't think she could stand another lie.

They traveled through the dense jungle all day, swatting away buzzing insects and burning in the sweltering heat despite the shade of the trees. The only good part of the journey seemed to be that there were rivers everywhere, which turned out to be clean sources of water. They stopped often, and when the sun started to set, they set up camp next to a babbling brook.

When the sun had all but disappeared, Ruby helped Dirk set up the tent in silence. Exhaustion had slowly seeped into her bones, and her feet hurt from walking and tripping over vines. She crawled into the tent once it was done and fell asleep immediately, staying as far away from Dirk as she could.

Something strange happened. She felt the world drop out from under her for the briefest of moments, as though she had simply fallen through the ground. Waking with a start, she found that everything was the same, except when she sat up, her body was still on the ground behind her.

Panic set in when she wondered if she had somehow died in the night. She turned to her body and tried to shake it. Her hands went right through, but she noticed her chest rising and falling. It was as though she was a ghost...

If she wasn't dead, then this was the strangest dream she had ever had.

Ruby couldn't help but notice how small and fragile her body looked there, curled up without a blanket. Even in sleep, she was sweating, and her eyelashes flickered as she dreamed. It was the most surreal experience she'd ever had. None of it felt right—her stomach felt queasy.

A light glowed outside. It grew brighter, illuminating the inside of the tent. Ruby glanced at Dirk. He was sound asleep, completely unaware of how unnatural the situation was, which meant the light was for Ruby.

Maybe she really had died, and her body just wouldn't stop breathing until she went to the light.

The great question had been solved, then—she would never get her answers.

When she stepped out of the tent, she stumbled backwards and fell through the tent wall. She laid there for a moment, uncertain of what she had seen. After her pounding heart slowed, she got back to her feet and walked through the tent once more.

In front of her was a dragon. He was the blinding white that had shone through Ruby's tent, and she was in awe. He had a magnificent scaled body with pure power rippling underneath his skin. His horns curled high into the air, beautiful and deadly. His nostrils flared, and his eyes glowed golden—there were no pupils or irises, just a brilliant gold. He hovered just above the ground, his massive wings sending leaves and twigs scattering away as gales of wind pummeled the dirt. His tail lashed out behind him, a faint flame at the end of it, though Ruby guessed it could ignite into much more than that if the dragon willed it to.

"Why have you come to my island?" the dragon asked in a deep voice that resonated through Ruby's bones. She felt faint.

Ruby felt compelled to tell the truth, and though she figured it was an effect of the dragon's presence, she tried to resist.

"To kill you," she answered in a trembling voice.

The dragon huffed, sending a stream of smoke through the air. "You are being used, my child."

Ruby shook her head. "I don't want to believe that," she said honestly. "I can't afford to believe that—this is a trade. The king promised me answers."

"I will give them to you freely," the dragon rumbled.

"I don't trust you. All anyone does is lie to me. How do I know you are no different?"

"I do not lie. I promise you answers, but you must work with me in order to get them."

"That's what the king said!" Ruby cried. "And I'm here on your island to kill you because of him! I'll die if I don't get the scales."

"That is no matter, child. All you need to do is open your mind. Cast your existence beyond this foolish quest you were sent on and remember."

Ruby tried. She really did—she closed her dream eyes and thought hard—but it was like there was a wall in between the memories she could access and the memories she couldn't. "I can't," she admitted in defeat.

"Yes, you can." The dragon closed his own eyes. "You were sent to kill a dragon before, and you spared her. She is on your land with a nest full of babies. You took five scales from her, and you left her, even though you knew that your defiance could have meant your death." The dragon gave Ruby a moment to think.

She listened to the words he said. She let them into her mind, and she imagined them, and they were no longer imagined—they were real. They were there, buried in the deep recesses of her mind, and she remembered what she had done, diving behind the nest so that the mother wouldn't blast her own children with fire before promising to take the scales and leaving her alone.

"I remember," Ruby gasped in awe. "Why did the mother trust me? Why did she let me leave instead of killing me?"

"Dragons communicate in many ways, child. She could hear your promise in your mind—she knew the situation could have been worse and decided to give up her scales so that no one had to die. She is pleased you spared her, and her babies are growing up quickly."

Ruby nodded. A headache appeared as the memories from the mother dragon on the mountain continued to return to her. "Why do they keep making me do this?" she asked. "How can I get out of this cycle?"

"You were born under a blood moon," the dragon said. "You are special, and your magic has always been sensed by others of strong power. The kingdom that imprisoned you had stolen you away from your parents and raised you to slay dragons. For a time, you learned willingly, but as you grew older and started to long for freedom outside of the kingdom, they started to fear you. They needed a way to control you, to use you for their needs, so they started taking your memories." The dragon sighed and looked down at the ground. "Killing dragons is dangerous, not only because we are dangerous beings, but because we are connected to many different realms beyond this world. When we die, that connection is severed, and the loss of that pours into the dragon slayer that killed them. Dragon slayers will go insane if they kill too many. You have killed before," the dragon claimed. "Can you remember?"

Ruby didn't want to, but she closed her eyes and imagined herself slaying a dragon. Then, just like before, it was a real memory. She saw herself at a slightly younger age, and she saw a younger version of Dirk. When she looked down at her feet, she saw a dragon, its wings slashed, scrabbling to get away from her past self.

She'd chased after it and killed it with a stab into the neck. It had been her very first victory, back when she believed dragons were evil. The kingdom had told her that dragons had killed her parents, and that lie had been a fresh source of vengeance.

At first, when she watched the dragon die, she'd felt satisfaction. She couldn't wait to tell Woodruff and the king, for them to be proud of her for becoming a killer at such a young age, but then, the feelings of loss had washed over her. She'd dropped the very same spear that was propped up in her tent and fell to her knees as overwhelming waves of grief battered her. Dirk had run to her side and had fallen to the ground next to her, cradling her in his arms. He sat there for hours, holding her and letting her cry. When he finally asked what was wrong, she told him.

For a while she had kept it together. But after each kill, Woodruff and the king had increasingly begun to worry that she was growing disobedient. And that was when they started taking her memories.

"How many have I killed?" Ruby asked after the memories had flooded back in. "Will I survive getting all of my memories back, or will I go insane?"

"You have killed five adult dragons and countless children," the dragon answered. He seemed to regret telling her this.

"I'm so sorry," Ruby whispered. At once the memories

came to her of the inherent goodness of dragons. Ruby had seen firsthand just how kind and wise they were. They were so very unlike the tales that were told across every kingdom. And so she apologized with every fiber of her being. She said it to both the dragon and the younger version of herself that was still in her mind. "I'm so sorry I believed them, that I listened to them and let them manipulate me for so long. If I hadn't…"

"This is not your fault, child," the dragon's voice was gentle.

"But I have killed so many."

"Only because you believed you were ridding the world of evil. You knew it was wrong the moment the very first dragon died, and you wanted to change things. It is not your fault that you did not understand that the real evil has been the one called Woodruff all along."

"Woodruff?" Ruby's eyes had started to water, but she wiped them away, scowling at the mere mention of his name. "What do you know of him? What about the king?"

"Woodruff has done a great amount of wrong in his life, but he is the only one who can give you answers—he is, after all, the one who butchered your mind in the first place. As for the king, he is oblivious to most of Woodruff's misdeeds. He has done you wrong and may seem trustworthy, but this is not solely because of his ignorance. Do not go to him for answers."

"And…Dirk?" Ruby asked hesitantly. The memory of him holding her still played through her mind.

"You may give him your trust. Everything he has done has been for your benefit. You almost died on Woodruff's order, and Dirk campaigned tirelessly for your cause. Ever since then, he has not risked anything that could get you killed. Do not give up on him." The dragon began to fade into the sky. "I must go—the timelines of dreams and timelines of reality go by very differently, and it is almost dawn."

"Wait! What do I do now?" Ruby pleaded desperately.

"That is a path only you can find," the dragon sounded distant, "and I am here to help you, so long as you can be helped."

Ruby watched the dragon fade. The winds his wings had created stopped suddenly, and everything was unnaturally still. Even the sun that Ruby hadn't realized was starting to rise seemed suspended in the air.

Ruby sat down and thought about everything that had just happened. She wasn't quite ready to wake up. Instead, she tried to remember more.

Still, there were walls around certain memories that she could feel were important. She tried to imagine more dead dragons, but without the white dragon's presence in her dream, she felt powerless to do so. No other memories returned to her.

She returned to her tent and paused to look down at her body. She had moved the tiniest bit closer to Dirk, as though she wanted to be nearer to him. Perhaps her subconscious in the dream and her re-emerging affection for Dirk had affected her physical body. He was on his side, facing her, and his eyes were open. He looked at Ruby's sleeping face with a sorrowful expression that somehow held a world of love in it as well.

Ruby wanted to sit down and watch the way he looked at her for forever. His lips pulled back into a flicker of a smile occasionally, and she wondered what he was thinking about. She wondered how painful it was for him to go through all of these years having to pretend as if he had never met her before. Knowing Woodruff, no doubt Dirk's family had been threatened. The nobleman would tolerate no deviation from the same routine that had yielded so much success already.

She imagined Dirk was exhausted, and suddenly, she felt horrible for the way she had treated him. She couldn't blame herself, she didn't know any better, but it was painful all the same.

Reluctantly, Ruby laid her dream body back down in her real one, and she was only truly asleep for a few moments before she opened her eyes to the real world.

SPEAR VERSUS DAGGER

*R*uby didn't mention her dream to Dirk. She wanted to tell him so badly, but knowing him and how protective he was of her, he'd only stress himself out about not being able to do anything to help.

Even though it killed her, she stayed quiet, acting like she had yesterday to keep him from becoming suspicious of her. Dirk would need a good reason to risk the safety of his family, kept hostage by Woodruff to ensure the squire kept the quests running smoothly. Before she told Dirk anything of what she knew now, she needed a plan that would work. More importantly, she would need to talk to them away from the crew of the Renegade, which might include some of Woodruff's spies.

The plan came to her as they walked deeper into the jungle, towards the center where the dragon was supposed to be. She needed to get Dirk's attention, and then she needed to keep it. She knew exactly what to do.

Slowing and purposefully falling behind, Ruby let him take the lead for a while. Then, she snuck up behind him until she was nearly pressed against his back, and she pushed him against a tree. He grunted at the sudden impact and immediately drew his sword. Ruby could see the surprise in his eyes when he realized it was just her and not an actual assailant. He put his sword back in its sheath, but Ruby didn't miss the way he kept his hand on the hilt.

"What are you doing?" he asked.

"Who am I, Dirk? What do you know about me?" she demanded.

"You know I can't tell you," he pleaded. He pushed against her and tried to move away from the tree, but Ruby shoved him harder and pointed her spear at his neck.

"I'll kill you if you don't tell me," she lied.

"Do it, then," he said. "I'll tell you nothing. Maybe, one day, you'll realize that all I've done has been for your own good. I don't care whether I return or not, and neither does Woodruff—he needs you more than he needs me."

Ruby backed away from him, but she held his gaze. When she was a few paces away, she rested the tip of her spear against her own neck.

"Don't come anywhere near me, or I'll do it!" she cried when he started forward. He immediately stopped. "Tell me who I am."

"Ruby, I can't!" Dirk protested. He took a step forward, and she pressed her spear harder against the side of her neck. She felt the warm trickle of blood, and Dirk fell to his knees. "Ruby, please, stop. He has my family hostage, Ruby."

"The dragon told me that everything you've done has been to protect me, and I know he was right, but regardless of that, all you've done is lie to me. I need the truth, Dirk, and this is your choice. You tell me everything, and I live. You don't, and I die."

"The dragon?" Dirk asked. Ruby knew he was stalling, but she answered him anyways.

"He visited me in my sleep. He gave me some of my

memories back, but not all of them. He said you would die to protect me, and I know he was right, so what's so difficult about simply telling the truth to keep me alive?" Ruby paused. "I need to break this cycle."

"Don't you get it?" Dirk screamed, raw panic in his voice. "You can't, Ruby! Woodruff will always be one step ahead of us. He'll suspect that you have your memories, and he'll do worse than make you keep drinking the potion if he finds out all you've learned! Knowing is going to kill you!"

"Then it kills me!" Ruby snapped. "I will not go on living if you don't tell me the truth, Dirk."

Ruby watched him give in. She watched his face change, and she listened to what he said.

"I am always the squire to a dragon slayer," he said quietly. "Everyone before you has either gone insane or died. Woodruff realized that killing dragons drove the dragon slayers so insane that they couldn't function, so he started experimenting with a mind erasure potion. He hasn't found a permanent solution, which is why it's so easy for bits and pieces to come back to you. Still, you forget enough, and that's all he wants." Dirk paused. "Training a dragon slayer is costly, both in time and in money. When they die after only three or four kills, that training becomes worthless. That's why he started dabbling in dark magic."

"How long have I been hunting dragons?" Ruby asked, even though she dreaded the answer.

"For two years. You became the focus of the kingdom, and you became my dragon slayer, and I, your squire." Dirk shook his head. "Every week for the past two years, I've had to pretend not to know you, and it's been so difficult. Every time, you're just as pleasant as the last—save for this time.

He took a deep, shuddering breath. "You break my heart, Ruby, every single time you're forced to forget, and I keep letting you, because even if I'm supposed to pretend like I don't know you, I'd rather have that than not have you in my life."

Ruby could barely speak. "Why did you want to be a squire in the first place?"

"When I told you that I wanted to become a knight, that was true."

Ruby looked at the ground. "If you wanted to be a knight for this kingdom, you're just as evil as Woodruff."

Dirk bit his lip. "Once a squire becomes a knight, he is allowed to pledge his allegiance to another friendly kingdom if he wishes. That, I believe, is the only way to get away from Woodruff."

"He's never going to make you a knight, is he?" Ruby asked sadly.

"I've never let myself believe that," he sighed.

"How many others are doing what I'm doing?"

"There are children in training, now that the memory potion has worked on you, but you're the only active dragon slayer."

Ruby didn't say anything. Dirk hadn't told her very much, but he'd told the truth, and that was worth something. As long as he knew that working for that kingdom was wrong, and that lying to her was useless, it was enough.

"Who is the man with the purple eyes?" Ruby asked tiredly.

"Another dragon slayer," Dirk replied, "the only one who went insane and still lives. He is chained up to keep him from harming himself. I think Woodruff only keeps him around because he's a good test subject. None of Woodruff's potions have worked on him because the man had been driven so far beyond insanity that there doesn't seem to be any going back, but Woodruff keeps trying. He's not going to stop until he makes something that works on that man."

Ruby nodded and pulled her spear away. Dirk got to his

feet and approached her. Ruby let him wrap his arms around her, and she wrapped hers around him in return. He needed this more than she did, and she let him have his moment.

"We need to complete this quest, or they'll kill both of us," Ruby said, "but I have a plan: we get the scales from the dragon, who promised that he would help me. I'll take them, but I won't kill him. We'll go back to the kingdom with the scales in hand, and Woodruff will give me the potion, but I won't drink it."

Dirk pulled away and stared at Ruby as if he thought she was insane. "Woodruff would find out and kill us."

"Not if we get away, Dirk. It's the only thing we've got."

Dirk didn't answer for a while. "Okay, it's worth a shot."

"Thank you for being honest with me," Ruby clasped his hands in hers, "and I'm sorry for all the pain I put you through."

"I can't even begin to understand what losing your memories is like, but I just always assumed it was better than remembering."

Ruby nodded, and they both started walking again. Ruby carried their rations in a sack while Dirk carried the chest of armor. Everything was just as exhausting as yesterday, but it didn't seem so bad, now that she finally felt like she could talk to Dirk.

"You said the dragon visited you in your dream," Dirk began.

"Yes. He had to leave before he could unlock all of my memories, but he told me enough, about how evil Woodruff is and how oblivious the king is."

"I don't know the king very well, even though I was friends with his son, but it wouldn't surprise me if Woodruff was really the one behind every decision the king has made so far."

"So, everything you told me about Channing and Mara was true?"

"Yes. I know Mara didn't kill Channing."

"Was she a dragon slayer?"

"No. At least, not that I know of."

Ruby stopped. "Are you certain, Dirk? Because maybe she did kill Channing, but she was just insane."

Dirk looked at Ruby, his eyes wide. "No, I would have known if she had killed dragons. She was never gone for days at a time, like we were."

"What if she was just one of Woodruff's test subjects?"

"But…why would he choose her?" Dirk asked. "I won't believe that Woodruff is responsible for both Channing's and Mara's death. He's evil, but he wouldn't have done that—the king would never have kept him around."

"Like I said, the king is oblivious," Ruby theorized. "Who knows what else Woodruff has done beyond keeping my memories buried?"

Dirk started walking again. "I won't believe anything until I get answers that make sense."

Ruby gave him a pointed look.

He noticed and glanced over at her. "What?"

"Do you get it now?" Ruby asked softly. "Do you understand what it was like to know everyone was lying to me, and no one would even bother to hide it?"

Dirk nodded. "I really am sorry."

He used his sword to cut through the thick vines that were in their path. Ruby held the chest while he worked, and she handed it back to him when the path was clear again.

Dirk stopped in his tracks and suddenly dropped the chest to the side, drawing his sword. Ruby hefted her spear in preparation to use it, but she couldn't see the source of his alarm.

Peeking around him, she saw a small clearing where little

huts stood, and other small structures made of wood and vines were positioned in a ring around a campsite. Humans that weren't quite humans had been walking around, but they stopped when they saw Ruby. All of them had weapons tucked into the grass clothing they wore, and they drew them immediately.

Ruby got a closer look at them when they charged at her and Dirk. They had snake-like eyes and green, scaly skin. Long tails stretched behind them— they looked more like giant, walking lizards than humans.

Ruby got ready to face them, as did Dirk. She didn't have her armor on, so they were both quite vulnerable.

Spear versus dagger gave Ruby some extra time to strike before the lizards reached her. Two fell to the ground, holes in their hearts, but more kept coming. Ruby did her best to dodge their close-range swipes and used her spear to block them, shoving them backwards.

Dirk seemed to be struggling a little bit less. His sword matched the daggers better as he could use it in close combat, but it was too difficult to fight them off when they were overwhelmed by their numbers.

"Stop!"

The voice was throaty and crackling. The lizards listened immediately—the three that had surrounded Ruby backed away, as did the two that had pinned Dirk down and were ready to kill him.

"Tend to the wounded," the voice said, and Ruby helped Dirk to his feet. They walked into the clearing and saw the lizard that spoke—he was dressed in more clothes than the others, and he had a thin vine wrapped around his head. He carried a staff with a brilliant jewel on the top. "I will see to the strangers."

"Who are you?" Dirk asked cautiously. Around them, the other lizards seemed to act like Ruby and Dirk weren't even there as they gathered the dead and helped the ones that survived.

"I am Kama'kio, the sage of this tribe." He dipped his head. "I apologize for the way my tribe greeted you—we are not accustomed to strangers and tend to answer their curiosity with aggression."

"Why did you stop them?" Ruby asked.

"The dragon of our island foretold your arrival. Come with me." Kama'kio turned and walked across the clearing. Ruby and Dirk exchanged wary glances before following him.

They went through a tunnel full of huge leaves and thick vines, and more of the same was carved into a giant stone slab at the end of the clearing. When they emerged, they were greeted by an impressively large city.

Houses made of stone stretched as far as Ruby could see. Intricate carvings she didn't understand made them look even more beautiful, and sprinkled between the regular houses were pyramid-like temples. In the middle of the city, a giant dragon carving stood proud, as if it was there to watch over all of the city's inhabitants.

"Welcome to the city of Malieu," Kama'kio said. "You entered our sick and wounded camp—we keep them isolated from Malieu, so that disease doesn't spread, and the injured are not tempted to go on with their lives as normal."

"This is so...advanced." Ruby looked around as they walked toward the dragon statue. It looked just like the dragon that had visited Ruby's dream.

"We have worked hard to create our city," Kama'kio told them. "The dragon showed us the ways of fire. It was because of his mercy that we survived, so now, we dedicate our lives to him. Everything we hunt, we offer him a portion of it. Everything we drink, we sprinkle on his shrine. Every new life is blessed by him, and every dead one is taken to one of his other realms." Ruby remembered how the dragon had told her that every one of his kind had connections beyond this world.

"Incredible," Dirk breathed.

Kama'kio brought them to the dragon shrine. There was a stone door at the bottom of it, and Kama'kio slid it upwards and held it so that Ruby and Dirk could enter before he did.

The room was giant and empty except for a fire in the middle.

"This is where I sleep when I must speak with him," Kama'kio said. "The fire is of his making, and it burns eternally. Through it, he can sense any presence that enters this sacred place. He can hear us now, if he chooses."

"How does he reach you?" Ruby asked. "You said he told you of our coming."

"I left my necklace in the fire. Once, it was attached to this emerald." He tipped his staff down to show them the glittering gem seated at the top. "Now that the chain is in the fire and the jewel on my staff, if the fire burns brighter, the jewel becomes brighter. That is how I know he wishes to speak with me."

"What did he tell you?"

"He spoke of more foolish humans that had come to kill him." Kama'kio shook his head. "Your kind is too greedy. Your kind wants everything, even if they have more than the rest of the creatures combined. They simply do not stop."

"What do the humans want with dragon scales?" Ruby asked. "That is my quest—to take the dragon's scales and leave."

"They want nothing of the dragon scales," he answered bitterly. "They do nothing for anyone. The dragon came to me one day when he was younger and had been hunted for the first time. I found a single dragon scale beside the fire. He asked me to study it, to search for properties within it that the humans could use, and I found nothing. It is no more than a ploy to kill more dragons, to keep them from breeding and expanding their kind, simply because the humans do not understand beings greater than them. There is no reason behind your quest but fear, and fear is a dangerous thing. Some humans have stolen dragons rather than killed them and kept them as pets. They enslaved the greatest creatures in the world and subdued them—there is no crueler race than your kind."

"I want to put an end to it," Ruby said, a single tear rolling down one of her cheeks. She turned to Dirk. "Did you know they were capturing dragons?"

"No," he said, stunned. "I've never seen a dragon beyond the ones I've been sent on quests to find."

"I have to see the dragon of this island," Ruby looked back at Kama'kio.

"You may call to him." Kama'kio gestured towards the fire.

"I need the scales," Ruby said. "The dragon promised that he would help me—I must see him in person beyond a vision in the flames."

"Very well," Kama'kio said, "though I will not tell you where to find him— that is not something I can do. If he wishes for you to find him, put something of value to you in the flames, as I did with the emerald."

"I have nothing," Ruby frowned, looking down at her meager possessions.

"That is untrue. Everyone has something. You may take your time. I will be here, meditating."

Kama'kio walked away, and Ruby looked helplessly at Dirk. "What do I do?"

Dirk seemed to be at a loss for words. "I don't know."

Ruby paced as she thought, glancing over at where Kama'kio sat. Then, she had an idea.

"My armor," she said, "is it still in the sick camp?"

"I think so," Dirk said.

"Stay here. I'm going to get it." She left the shrine without waiting for Dirk to answer and hurried back through the tunnel. At first, it was disorienting trying to weave her way back through the city, and she worried she was going in the wrong direction when she finally reached the sick camp.

Her chest was at the opposite end of the clearing. She ignored the lizards tending to the hurt and the sick and rummaged through the chest until she found the breastplate.

The sides were still melted slightly. She ripped the worn leather by tearing it from the rest of the armor and rushed back to the shrine, where Dirk leaned against one of the walls. When he saw Ruby, he smiled.

"Good idea," he chuckled, following Ruby as she went to the fire.

"You're not going to be worried that Woodruff will be upset about this?" she asked.

"On the contrary, I can't wait to spite him." Dirk grinned widely as Ruby dropped the piece into the fire

Ruby sat down in front of the fire the same way Kama'kio did. She put her feet and her hands together. Closing her eyes, she thought hard about the dragon and the armor, willing for him to visit her.

She waited for a long time, but nothing happened.

REPTILIAN EYES

"I don't think it's working," Ruby said to Dirk after a while.

"Are you sure?" Dirk asked.

"Yes. I don't sense his presence, and he has a strong one."

"Maybe it's not the armor, then," Dirk mused, moving to sit down next to Ruby.

"I don't know what else it could be."

"Think, Ruby." Dirk took her hands, and she looked up at him. "We didn't come this far for you to give up."

"I could just force an answer out of Kama'kio," she said jokingly.

"Ruby, seriously."

"I was kidding!"

"We don't have time for jokes. You've got to think."

Ruby did, but it was hard to focus with Dirk's warm hands clasped around hers. She remembered how it felt to be held by him, and she wanted that more than anything, even though she was supposed to be figuring out how to get to the dragon.

"I know what it is!" Ruby exclaimed. "Do you still have your lock pick?"

"My lock pick?" Dirk felt around in his pockets for it. "Why would it be my lock pick?"

"My memories came back briefly in between our last dragon and this one," Ruby confessed. "Things were coming back because my emotions for you were stronger than anything else I'd felt, so the potion didn't work correctly. Woodruff had your lock pick—I used it to get away, and that's when I saw the man with the purple eyes."

"It's sentimental to you because of me?" Dirk asked, his voice soft.

"Yeah," Ruby said with a smile. "Do you have it?"

He pulled it out of his pocket. "I'm honored that it's sentimental to you, but it's also sentimental to me. I've had it since my childhood." Dirk winced. "I can't believe I'm getting rid of it."

"Sorry," Ruby said, staring at the lock pick.

"What if it doesn't work, and I gave it up for nothing?" he asked anxiously.

"It'll work, Dirk—I promise." Ruby held out her hand. Dirk moved to place it in her palm, then pulled it away again. "Dirk, we have to finish this mission. Come on."

"Okay, okay." Dirk gave her the lock pick, and she dropped it in the fire before meditating again. As soon as she closed her eyes, she saw him—the dragon.

"Take the path through the city and find the crater," he said in the same voice that Ruby remembered from her dream. "Find the darkest entrance and go through it. You will find me in the deepest cavern, and I will help you."

Before Ruby could say anything, the dragon faded. She opened her eyes to Dirk frantically shaking one of her shoulders.

"Ruby!" he yelled desperately.

"I got the answer," Ruby said, confused. "Why are you so concerned?"

"Your eyes glowed golden," he sunk down to his knees. "I thought something went wrong."

"They did?" Ruby asked, moving a hand over one of her eyes.

"That happens when a dragon connects to your soul."

Ruby moved her hand and saw Kama'kio approaching. "His soul needs a place to connect to yours, and often, it is through the eyes."

"I know how to find him," Ruby said. "We should really be off, but thank you for helping us."

"You should stay until morning," Kama'kio smiled. "It's getting late."

When Ruby lifted the stone slab, she found the sun sinking. "Time goes by differently in dreams and memories," she realized out loud. "It's okay—we really should be off as soon as we can."

"There are things in the night that you do not want to encounter," Kama'kio warned.

"How far away is the crater?"

"Far enough to make it a dangerous journey. I suggest you wait until morning. As for tonight, the moon is full—the dragon is at his strongest, and we will celebrate him." Kama'kio led them around to a grass clearing behind the shrine.

Various fires seemed to be burning on the ground, though they were controlled. Around them, the inhabitants of the city sat and meditated or danced, glowing in the face of the flames.

Ruby sat outside the ring and watched. The way the dancers moved was beautiful and raw—she was glad to witness this, to see a civilization untouched by humans and still full of more respect than humans had ever possessed.

The night became darker, and Ruby grew tired. She and Dirk sat in a comfortable silence, watching the celebration, and despite her best attempts to stay awake, her eyes drifted closed.

"Do you want to sleep?" Dirk asked her. "I can set up our tent."

Ruby yawned and nodded. Dirk left her there, and she tried to stay awake, but her eyes kept closing.

"Seeing the dragon has drained you," Kama'kio had come up to her after spending his time dancing. He stretched out a hand. "Before you sleep, you should honor him—dance with us."

Ruby took his hand, and he helped her to her feet before leading her to one of the flames.

"I don't know how to dance," she confessed. "I wouldn't want to impose."

"You are doing no such thing. Just follow the flames around the fire, and dance." Kama'kio gracefully leaped forward and closed his eyes. He skipped more than danced, but it was primal and beautiful. Ruby took a deep breath and stared into the fire, following it the way he had said to, and in an instant, she could feel the dragon's presence.

It was strong in the flames. She even thought she saw his wings appear, and her movements started to feel right. She moved her arms gracefully and skipped the way Kama'kio did.

"You feel it," Kama'kio called to her. Ruby couldn't respond, she could feel the dragon's strength flowing through her, helping her remember even more. Many pieces were still missing, but she was getting there, and that was all that mattered.

When Ruby couldn't dance anymore, she retreated from the fire, a big smile on her face. Kama'kio nodded at her and kept dancing with his tribe. When Ruby turned, she saw Dirk standing there, staring at her in fascination.

"You moved just like them," he said as she walked towards him. "How?"

"He was there," she turned back to look at the flames. "He was in the fire—I felt him. He taught me to dance." Ruby stumbled into Dirk's arms, and he caught her.

"Are you alright?" he asked. She could feel his breath on her neck.

"I think the power made me dizzy," she murmured, "but it wasn't unpleasant."

She felt like she was spinning. She understood why the lizards kept up with this tradition, why they danced every full moon. It was more than worshipping the dragon—it was giving them power, and she supposed that Kama'kio had been surprised that a foreigner had felt that power too.

Dirk helped her into their tent, which he'd set up at the edge of the clearing. "I hope Kama'kio doesn't see this as disrespectful. What if we aren't supposed to have a tent set up in the clearing?"

"It's fine," Ruby said, laying down. "The dragon won't mind—only the shrine and the fires are sacred." She turned on her side to face Dirk, who climbed underneath the blankets. Ruby was happy, as if after all this time, everything was right. She would finish this mission without killing any dragons, and then, she would be free from Woodruff's grasp. The best part of it all was that Dirk would be by her side.

"Would you really go against the kingdom for me?" Ruby asked.

"I'll do everything I can to help," he said, facing her. "I swear that to you."

"Even at the cost of being a knight?"

"Maybe that's the wrong thing to do. I can't stop thinking about what Kama'kio said, about how we're greedy creatures.

I don't want to serve the king if he's taking dragons captive and killing the rest for no reason outside of fear."

Ruby nodded. "I'm glad."

She could still hear the feet pounding on the ground as the dance continued, and she heard their voices as they spoke and even sang. It was a comforting sound to fall asleep to, but there was one more thing Ruby wanted.

"Will you hold me again?" she asked Dirk. It was an uncomfortable question, but she bit her lip and waited for his response.

He nodded and opened his arms the same way he had before. She moved into them, and Dirk shifted onto his back so that her head was on his chest, and his arms were wrapped around her. She buried her head into the side of his neck and closed her eyes, relishing the warm feeling of protection that he gave her.

She slept peacefully and woke in the morning as the sun rose. Dirk had held her for the entire night.

Ruby looked up at him and stroked his cheek with her thumb, watching as his lips curled up in a small smile.

She wondered what they would feel like against hers.

His eyes fluttered open, and he looked at Ruby in contentment. He raised his arms to stretch and winced in pain.

"Is that from your fall?" Ruby asked, putting a gentle hand over his stomach.

He nodded. "I broke a few ribs and dislocated my shoulder," he said, his eyes distant as though he was reliving that day. "Woodruff healed me. His magic was the only reason I'd stayed alive—he had put a protection spell on me so that my chances of dying were lower. There are so few squires these days, and since we're close, he wanted to keep me paired with you so that there was someone with you that you trusted. I suppose he just never suspected I'd get to the point where you became more important to me."

"I'm glad you healed so quickly."

Dirk nodded. "Woodruff knows you didn't kill that dragon, so he took it out on me by not healing me completely."

"What?" Ruby asked, sitting up. "He knows?"

"I don't know how—I think he can sense the dragon's energy, the same way you can sense the dragon's presence here, so he knew he was losing his grip on you. You said his last potion made hatred your strongest emotion, so I think he expects different results this time."

"Well, he won't get them." Ruby crawled out of the tent, and Dirk followed her. There were two stone bowls sitting outside, a stone cover nestled over each of them. Ruby opened one, and Dirk opened the other. Inside were little pieces of meat mixed with greens and berries Ruby didn't recognize. A spoon sat against the side of both bowls.

"Cheers," Dirk said jokingly, tapping his bowl against Ruby's. They started eating, and Ruby was surprised by how delicious it was.

Footsteps sounded nearby, and Ruby looked up to see Kama'kio approaching.

"There is a stream that runs alongside the path to the crater. You can find fresh water there. The rations you brought with you were…broken into." Kama'kio held out Ruby's spear and Dirk's sword. "As for these, I managed to get them back."

"Thank you for everything, Kama'kio," Ruby bowed shallowly in respect. "We'll stop by again when we leave, and I'm sorry for our entrance."

"Creatures die—it is the way of life. You were afraid of being killed, so you fought back. I understand. My tribe is reckless sometimes, and I had not told them of your coming. Do not grieve them."

Ruby nodded, though in some small part of her mind, she would always grieve for those she had killed. Kama'kio turned and walked back to the shrine.

Ruby and Dirk took down their tent and bundled it as small as they could.

"What about your armor?" Dirk asked as they started to walk away.

"My dragon slaying days are over. I don't need it anymore." Ruby paused. "Unless you want to carry it all the way back to Woodruff?"

"No way," Dirk scoffed. "That chest put too much of a strain on my body. He can do without it."

"Good." They found the path they were looking for and walked along it. It was just dirt, so it wasn't really a path, but it was easy to follow, even as it wound around trees and more stone slabs.

"How long do you think these lizard people have existed?" Ruby asked. "Have you ever heard of them before?"

"We knew there were inhabitants on the island, but we assumed they were humans. They seem ancient," he thought aloud, running a hand over one of the stone slabs.

"Maybe they're descendants of the dragon. It would explain their scaly skin and reptilian eyes."

"That would make sense, though it's a strange thought," Dirk said.

"It is."

It didn't take long for them to find a stream to rest by. They'd taken the stone bowls with them, and after rinsing hers in the stream, Ruby filled it with fresh water and drank. Dirk did the same.

They didn't have to walk much longer to find the crater the dragon had told her about. It was an impressive size, and from their vantage point at the top, it felt as if they were standing on the top of a mountain and looking down at a valley. The crater was filled with trees, and all kinds of plants seemed to be flourishing in the vast jungle inside.

"What caused this?" Ruby asked.

"Perhaps the dragon will know and be willing to answer."

They both stumbled down the ridge of the crater. Ruby tripped over a small stone and bit back a curse as sharp branches whipped past her face. She was covered in scrapes by the time they reached the bottom. "Think we'll be able to get back up?" Dirk asked.

"I'm sure. If we can't, maybe the dragon will give us a ride."

"Somehow, I doubt he would be that benevolent," Dirk gave her a wry smile.

"I don't know, he's pretty great. I mean, he's taken care of the people here for so long, and he's willing to help me even after I killed other dragons." She paused and stopped walking. "What if it's a trap, Dirk? What if it's another lie?"

"Do you truly believe that?" Dirk asked.

"No, but I've trusted plenty of people who've lied to me."

"Ruby, I don't think he's lying. I think he truly wants to help you. Besides, we can't return to the kingdom without his scales, so we have to face him no matter what happens."

She nodded, and they pressed on. They found a dark tunnel, and Dirk started to enter it, but Ruby told him to stop. "What if this isn't the darkest one?" she asked cautiously.

"It looks pretty dark to me."

"I suppose we don't really have time to go around in search of other tunnels," Ruby said, thinking of her head-dress. Exploring the entire crater could take days, and they still had to get back to the ship and then from there, back to the kingdom. She walked forward, stepping into utter darkness.

She worried about finding her way down such a dark path when her hands started to glow. She looked down and realized it was the water in the bowl.

"How is it doing that?" Dirk asked, staring into his bowl with fascination.

"They're bioluminescent creatures," Ruby said with a smile. She looked over the entire bowl, careful not to spill what little water was left after their trek down the ridge. "Amazing. I didn't know they were anywhere but in the ocean."

"How did you know about them?" Dirk asked, holding his bowl out in front of him.

Ruby put hers next to it. "Devereux showed me." She took a step forward and looked back at Dirk. "Are you ready?"

"I don't think so," he said.

"Me neither."

But still, they walked forward.

TOO YOUNG TO DIE

*W*hen they got deep enough in the tunnel, Ruby started to see a familiar glowing white.

"That's him," Ruby said, quickening her pace. She rounded the corner towards the light and came to a stop— the dragon was even more magnificent in person.

He was curled up in the center of a giant cavern. Ruby would have thought he was asleep if one of his eyes didn't open.

"Woah," Dirk said, and he took an involuntary step back. "In all of our quests to search for dragons, I've never seen one like this."

The dragon rose to his feet and approached Ruby and Dirk. She blinked, and her vision was warped just enough for her to realize this was some sort of dream state, similar to a real dream. When she stepped away from her body, she turned and saw that her eyes really were golden.

"You have come for my scales," he rumbled, dipping his head so that it was directly in front of Ruby.

She stared into his wise eyes.

"Yes," she responded quietly. It didn't feel right to look

directly at such an ethereal being. She could feel his power pulsing off his enormous body, and she swallowed back the rising tide of fear within her.

"Very well. You may take them."

The dragon lifted his head to expose his chest. Ruby's vision was no longer warped—she was seeing the dragon normally, now that there was nothing left for either of them to say.

She turned back to Dirk.

"We can take a few scales," she said quietly. He nodded and handed Ruby his sword.

Ruby approached the dragon until she was right in front of him. She looked up into his eyes, which flickered down to hers. Then, the dragon dipped his head and shut his eyes, indicating that he knew there would be pain.

Ruby gave him a nervous nod in return and pried off the scales as quickly as she could. Every time the dragon flinched, she started to pull away, but she gritted her teeth and remembered that she had to get this done.

Blood pooled over the skin underneath after she had extracted three scales. The dragon bowed his head and licked at the minor wound. Ruby returned to Dirk with tears in her eyes. She stopped and glanced back once more at the dragon.

"I will never kill another dragon—I swear it, and I swear to do my best to free the others that can be freed," she promised. The dragon paused for a moment and dipped his head again. Ruby turned and walked out of the tunnel without saying anything.

"I didn't know dragons could be like that," he said, awe lingering in his voice. "That one was huge and radiating power, and I thought it was going to kill us, but it didn't."

"He."

"What?"

"It's a he."

"Did you speak to him at all?" Dirk bombarded Ruby with his questions. He was still shaken after the encounter with the dragon.

"Yes, for a moment. He just told me to take the scales—that's all."

"I've never spoken to a dragon."

"You didn't mind leading me to kill them," Ruby said coldly. "How could you let me do that?"

"Ruby, both of our lives were in danger," Dirk pleaded. "There is nothing I can do but apologize for the past and move on. I am sorry, but there's still a chance to do better. I messed up, but you're not blameless either."

Ruby didn't answer. She didn't want to argue about the same things anymore, because Dirk was right. There was nothing either of them could do to change the past. They just had to keep going forward.

"We'll make our difference now," Ruby decided. "We'll trick Woodruff. I'll keep my memories, and we'll keep helping the dragons."

"That doesn't sound like much of a plan."

"It doesn't? What were you thinking? We take down the whole kingdom?" Ruby almost laughed.

"Yes, actually," Dirk said, scratching his head. "I mean, think about it. We'll have the dragons on our side, and we should get his help and burn everything down in that kingdom. We could start over."

"What happened to doing better, Dirk?" Ruby asked.

"You don't think Woodruff and the king deserve to pay for what they've done?" he asked as they made their way across the crater.

"No, I do, but we can't burn down a whole kingdom just because of them. There are too many innocent people. If we get rid of Woodruff and the king, we should do it quietly and efficiently. For now, we stick to helping the dragons."

Suddenly, the bushes in front of them rustled, and Ruby backed away before lifting her spear, but it was Kama'kio who stepped out. He was barely even startled by the sight of her spear.

"Ruby," he said, uncharacteristically out of breath, "there is another human who has come to the island. He is after the dragon—he's attacking our village!"

"What? Did he say who he was?" Ruby felt a surge of worry that Woodruff was on to her, and that he sent someone after her to make sure she got the job done.

"No, but he seems regretful, like he does not want to do this, but he has to," Kama'kio responded.

"I'll be there in a moment, but I have to talk to the dragon before I face him. Can you and your tribe hold him off?" Ruby asked.

"Yes, but he is very demanding. He doesn't seem to have anything to lose—too many of my people have been injured already."

Without another word, Kama'kio dashed off in the direction he'd come from.

"We can't go all the way back to the dragon's lair!" Dirk looked at Ruby like she was crazy. "We've got to help!"

"Go, then." Ruby sat down and closed her eyes. "I'll be fine here. If I can meditate, I think I can reach him."

Dirk looked like he wanted to stay, but Ruby heard his footsteps crash through the dense brush as he followed the path back to the village.

Ruby focused on her breathing. She mimicked what Kama'kio had done inside of the temple, but nothing seemed to happen. Still, she stayed exactly how she was. She imagined the dragon, imagined him coming into her dream, and eventually, he did.

She opened her eyes into the dreamscape to see him

landing on the ground in front of her. "There is a man here for you," she hurried to say. "Who is he?"

The dragon closed his eyes and nodded. "Masellico Vyrens. Another dragon slayer, much like you. He is younger by a few years—I can sense his life force. He has killed before and is so afraid of dying that he continues to do so. That is the weakness the man who manipulated you holds over him —the knowledge that he does not want to die."

"Does he have his memories, or is he losing them too?"

"He has his memories, but he is no less a pawn of your human kingdom than you are."

"Can I save him?" Ruby asked as she clambered to her feet.

The dragon paused as though he was thinking about his answer. "I do not know," he murmured. "That is a fate for you to decide. I have no control over the future."

Ruby opened her eyes to reality and surged to her feet, clutching her spear. She ran after the tracks both Kama'kio and Dirk had left, sending silent hopes that it wasn't too late for Masellico. If he was like her, then there had to be hope.

She emerged into the city after crawling up the crater. The lizard men rushed back and forth in a panic. She headed toward the commotion and found Dirk fighting a man who was much taller and broader than him.

Dirk didn't seem to have any advantage against a bigger and more agile opponent. He spent most of the fight narrowly avoiding blows that could have ended his life and seemed to realize he had to do more.

He leapt up onto one of the stone buildings while the man chopped at where Dirk had just been with his axe. Dirk landed on the handle and kicked the man hard in the face, sending him flying backwards while Dirk stumbled to the ground. He looked up and met Ruby's gaze. He pointed, and

Ruby followed his finger to where another man was hacking at the lizard men surrounding him.

Ruby jumped into the fray. Dirk could handle himself, and she was guessing that it was her fault that Masellico had followed her here, so he was her problem to deal with, not the lizard men that dwelled on the island.

He seemed surprised to see Ruby. She attacked him ruthlessly, and he met every single blow, so Ruby kept pushing. She dove to the ground to avoid his sword and spun, punching behind Masellico's legs so that he stumbled forward. Ruby swept her leg underneath him, tripping him even more. Then, she struck a blow with the back of her spear to the side of his neck, rendering him unconscious.

She felt a small pang of guilt as she squatted in front of him, looking him over for any serious injuries. He was bleeding in a few places, but they seemed to be minor scratches.

Kama'kio approached him and lifted his staff, preparing to bring it down.

"No!" Ruby yelled, but Kama'kio brought it down anyway. Ruby laid her body across the man's chest and held her spear up just in time to catch the bottom of the staff.

"What are you doing?" Kama'kio asked in surprise.

"He is not yours to kill!" Ruby snarled.

"Very well. You kill him."

"No! He can be saved."

Kama'kio lifted his staff and pulled it away while Ruby went on. "I was like him, being used as Woodruff's pawn. I'm not the same anymore." She pulled the dragon scales out from a hidden pocket in the seam of her pants and showed them to Kama'kio. "Two years ago, I would have slain a dragon for these. Now, I'm working to save them. If I could change, he can too."

"Are you sure?" Dirk asked, approaching Ruby. Behind

him, the man he'd been fighting was sprawled out on the ground. "It's not a good idea to let him live."

"You let me live for years!" Ruby retorted. She still hovered near Masellico. "Why not him? Because you don't love him?"

Dirk flinched.

"He deserves a chance."

Dirk just walked away. The lizards followed him—Kama'kio was the last—and Ruby stayed with Masellico until he woke up.

"Hi," Ruby said, tucking her dragon scales into her pocket before Masellico could see them. He looked at her and squinted.

He tried to grab for his sword, but Ruby had kicked it away when he was first knocked out.

"Don't kill me!"

"I'm not going to," Ruby reassured him, doing her best to look sympathetic, "but in return, you have to promise me something." Ruby paused, and Masellico nodded. He looked so innocent, with his smooth skin and wide eyes. He stared up at Ruby in anticipation. "You can't kill the dragon on this island."

His eyes became impossibly wide. "I have to," he said, his voice trembling. "For Torbek."

Ruby studied him. "You trained as a dragon slayer?"

He nodded. "The man in purple will kill me if I don't bring back the dragon scales," he said. "I have to kill the dragon."

Ruby opened her pouch and showed him the scales she had. His face was full of shock. "I didn't kill him, and I got the scales, Masellico. You can't kill him."

"Woodruff will know," he said, his eyes fixated on the scales. "He'll sense that the dragon is still alive, and he'll kill me anyways. I have to kill the dragon. Don't you get that?"

Ruby tried not to focus too much on the strong belief Masellico harbored that Woodruff knew the dragon lived. "Trust me, I do. I've been manipulated and brainwashed by our kingdom, by Woodruff, more than anyone else. He stole my memories and has sent me on the same two quests every time I've woken up again, so that killing the dragons won't drive me crazy. I found a way to beat him, okay? I won't let him kill you."

"You can't stop him!" Masellico sat up suddenly and punched Ruby in the jaw. Ruby reeled, and Masellico snatched up his sword. "You'll have to kill me to stop me."

Ruby stood, her spear in hand. "I could have killed you, but I didn't. We can get through this. We can get out of this—you just have to trust me, okay?"

"How can I, when you turn against Torbek like this?" Masellico jabbed his sword at her, and Ruby dodged to the side.

"Is Torbek's system really what you want to fight for?" Ruby didn't bother explaining that it wasn't her kingdom. "They steal dragons and kill them or keep them as pets. How can you not find that horrible?"

"It doesn't matter what I find horrible! All that matters is that I return with dragon scales from a dead dragon. I'm too young to die."

"Then why do you fight me?" Ruby asked softly. She didn't strike—she only blocked or dodged Masellico's blows. "You won't win this."

"You've lost your killing edge. I'll show you how a dragon slayer fights!" Masellico went for Ruby's left and turned at the last second to strike at Ruby's right. Pain lanced through her side, and she sucked in a pained breath as she touched it and felt the warm trickle of her blood.

She didn't want to give up on Masellico, but she wouldn't die to save him.

Ruby tried to ignore the burning pain. She was slower and weaker on that side—she could see Masellico calculating that advantage right before he struck.

When he did, she was ready. She fell to the ground on her left so that Masellico missed, and within moments, she rolled onto her back before jumping to her feet. Masellico turned just in time.

"Give up, please," Ruby begged. "This is your last chance, Masellico, I don't want to kill you."

"Stop saying my name!" His voice cracked, but he kept attacking, and Ruby began to understand him. He hurt more when he killed something he knew was as sentient as him.

"Do you know how I know it?" Ruby asked, blocking and dodging his next few swings. "The dragon told me—the very dragon you want to kill. His power spans realms, you know. He helps people and creatures alike, and he hurts every time another dragon is killed. He can sense you on this island right now—your life force, your rage, and a lot more about you. He is great and powerful. He is needed by this world."

Masellico's attacks became slower and sloppier. Ruby landed a few blows with the back of her spear, and Masellico started to tire.

"I know what you're doing! You're trying to make me feel bad, but it won't work!" Masellico's strength seemed to return. He charged at Ruby, pressing his sword up against her spear. She pushed him away, but Masellico was ready, so at the last minute, she leapt up over him and impaled him with her spear.

She sank to her knees when she realized she'd dealt a fatal wound.

He fell onto his stomach. Ruby pulled her spear out and rolled him over. He was struggling to breathe—blood dripped out of the corner of his mouth while tears pooled in his eyes.

"I'm sorry," Ruby whispered, stroking his curly hair back from his forehead. "I'm so sorry. You deserved a better life, and I wish you had let me give one to you."

"Thank you," he said, a tired smile on his face. "I don't have to kill anymore."

Those were his last words. He got one last breath out before his face went blank. Ruby could see the moment his soul left his body.

"Ruby?"

She looked up to see Dirk approaching her, and she didn't know if she could handle telling him what had just happened. She was grateful that she didn't have to when Dirk silently pulled her to his chest

ANXIOUS AIR

*R*uby and Dirk made their way back to the dock when the sun was at its peak in the sky. They found the crew sitting around and waiting.

"Are we ready to leave?" Ruby asked, clutching the pouch that held the dragon scales. Before she left, Kama'kio had tied a string to either end of her spear so that she could wear it slung over her back.

"Leave?" Devereux turned from where he was having a conversation with one of the crew members by the wheel. There was a coldness in his eyes and his voice. "We aren't going anywhere."

"What do you mean?" Ruby demanded. Her headdress had tightened over the days, and she didn't have very long to get back to Woodruff.

"There's a storm out there." Devereux nodded toward the open ocean. "Can't you see it?"

Ruby didn't want to admit that she did. The clouds over the horizon were grey and rumbling, rolling straight at the island. She looked at Dirk helplessly.

"When will we be able to sail?" he asked.

"I don't know, lad. Maybe in a day or two."

"I don't have that time!" Ruby marched right up to Devereux. "We leave now."

"No." Devereux stood and towered over her, staring her down. "I am captain of this ship, or have you forgotten your place again?"

Ruby backed down, but her eyes didn't leave his. "I know how you pirates settle things—with a duel. I challenge you to one. If I win, we sail now. If I lose, we wait."

Devereux laughed. "Firstly, duels only end in death, and they are to settle disputes. Only one lives. I need to get you back to that kingdom alive, which is why I will not sail right now. Secondly, you are bold to think you stand a chance against me." He was angry—Ruby could hear it in his trembling voice.

"Or maybe I'm desperate, because if I don't get back soon, I'll die anyways! So, you have two options—take me through that storm, and we have a chance at surviving. Stay here, and there's no chance for me. Woodruff will end you when he finds out you killed me!"

Some of the crew laughed in the background. Dirk put a steady hand on Ruby's shoulder while Devereux spoke.

"A couple more days on land isn't going to kill you."

"Yes, it will! See this headdress?" Ruby knocked on it, then tried to take it off with everything she had, but it only got tighter. "I can't take it off! It's getting tighter, and when enough time passes, it's going to kill me. You want to try?"

Devereux tried and failed. He couldn't get the piece off.

"Why would Woodruff kill you like this?"

"To make sure I come back," Ruby said, crossing her arms. She looked down at the floor. "I don't want to put your crew in danger, Devereux, but I need to go home. I need to find my way out of Woodruff's game. I can't die yet."

Devereux nodded silently for a moment, just staring at

Ruby. She felt strange under his gaze. Finally, he turned to his crew. "We sail now!" he bellowed. "Any who wish to not risk their lives in that storm may remain on this island, and I will return for you—pirate's oath." He tapped his left hand against his chest three times.

No one moved to leave the ship. Some immediately started manning the ropes. Another climbed up to the crow's nest, and many others went below deck to do whatever was necessary to prepare for their journey. Devereux had a pleased smile on his face as he went to the wheel. He yelled for the ship to be let go, so a few of the crew members jumped over the edge and into the water to unknot the ropes. The ship slowly drifted away from the island, and they pulled back to get a running start. Using the rope, they climbed their way up the side of the ship.

Within minutes, their journey began, right into the heart of the storm. Ruby stayed above deck, her eyes occasionally pulled to where Devereux was piloting the vessel. She wanted to talk to him, to make amends with him, but she wasn't quite sure how to do that.

"He'll forgive you, you know." Ruby turned to see Melody approaching her. Dirk had gone belowdecks a long time ago.

"I don't want to chance getting my head sliced off," Ruby murmured, looking back at Devereux.

Melody laughed. "He wouldn't do that." She stood next to Ruby and looked off at the sea. "Devereux's one of the only people in my life that I admire. He took me in as a crew member when I was little and living on one of these islands, actually. He came by one day, ready to loot, but my village was mostly women and children—our men were fighting a war with one of the other tribes on a different island. When he realized this, he gave instead of took. We had food, water, and even a few weapons to defend ourselves with. I begged him to teach me to use a sword. His eyes were always drawn towards the sea, like he wanted to leave, but instead of abandoning me, he gave me the choice to go with him."

"What about your mother?" Ruby asked quietly.

Melody shrugged. "I love her, but at that moment, when I was faced with a choice between freedom or to just wait and see if we were to become a part of the other tribe, I chose freedom. It was easier to leave than it would have been to find out. I still don't know what happened to any of them." Melody paused. "Anyway, that's not the point—it's Devereux. He respects those that deserve respect. He doesn't care about age—he respected me when I was little for wanting to learn. When you lashed out at him, he became cold towards you because he decided you no longer deserved his respect. Dare I say, he was right to."

"I know he was. I'm sorry to you too, Melody, for behaving like that—it was just so confusing and scary to have almost all of my memories just barely out of reach. I didn't even think I could trust Dirk, who's been there for me through everything, even when I didn't know it."

"I get that, I think." Melody's brows furrowed. "I see my island sometimes, and Devereux always asks me if I want to go back to it. I always say no, even though it's right there. The answers are in sight. The only difference is, I was too afraid. From the sound of it, you're chasing after the answers you need. That's something worthy of respect."

"I don't think he respects me. I think he pities me for my lack of freedom, but I'll show him. I'll free the dragons and take down Woodruff."

Melody smiled. "Tell him that, not me. Also, to let you in on a little secret, Devereux may go along with how Woodruff treats him like they're old friends, but Devereux really doesn't like Woodruff much."

Ruby nodded. "Thank you, Melody."

She nudged Ruby, and Ruby approached Devereux.

"Having a conversation with Melody, who should be working?" Devereux intentionally let the last part carry, and Melody just rolled her eyes and went back to work with the barest hint of a smile on her lips.

"I'm sorry, Devereux," Ruby frowned, "for everything. You're right—I do forget my place sometimes, and you didn't deserve to be caught up in my anger. I owe this entire journey to you."

"I'm glad you've come to your senses." Devereux sighed. "When you spoke about your headdress, I didn't believe you. I've never cared for Woodruff much, no more than exchanging simple pleasantries that are necessary for me to keep this job, but when you said that headdress is to make sure you return…" Devereux trailed off. "If there's one thing I can't respect, it's not allowing someone their freedom."

"I'm going to take him down, Devereux. I'm not sure how yet—my priority is freeing the dragons he's captured—but he will no longer be in any position to take anyone's freedom when I'm finished with him."

"You will have my help if you need it, but be careful. Woodruff will be watching you like a hawk."

"Aren't you going back out to sea after bringing me back to the kingdom?"

"Maybe I could convince the crew to dock for a little while." Devereux gave her a sly smile.

"Thank you, truly. Woodruff has caused a lot of harm to many others like me, and it stops now."

Ruby stayed next to Devereux as they approached the storm. The crew was getting nervous—the atmosphere was tense on the ship.

"Are you ready for this?" Devereux asked, his eyes steady on the storm. The waters were getting rougher below, and rain drizzled down on the ship.

"Yes, I'm ready," Ruby said, taking a deep breath.

"Devereux!" Melody came running up, ropes looped around both of her arms.

Devereux's expression turned grim. "You think we need ropes?"

"Lookout said it's rough out there—real rough. Renegade's about to list real bad."

Devereux nodded and took two of the ropes. "Take the wheel, Melody, while I secure Ruby." He went to the starboard railing and started looping the rope around it.

"What is this for?" Ruby asked.

"To make sure we stay with the ship," Devereux answered. He wrapped it around Ruby's waist next and tied a secure knot. He picked up one of the ends. "If this goes wrong, if the ship breaks and starts sinking, pull on this end."

Ruby nodded. "Good luck," she said.

Devereux gave her an answering nod and tied himself to the wheel before ordering Melody to bring Dirk up and secure him.

Melody was right, and Ruby stumbled as the ship tilted sharply to the side. Ruby tucked the shaft of her spear under her armpit as extra security and clutched onto the rail with one hand. Her other was holding protectively onto the pouch with the dragon scales.

"We're tying ourselves to the ship?" Dirk asked from behind Ruby.

"Yes," Melody said, securing him. The rest of the crew was secured as well—Melody was the last.

They all waited in quiet anticipation. Ruby lurched to the side as the ship bounced over the waves. A few times, her rope was what caught her and kept her from flying right over the edge. Devereux was struggling to captain, but Melody had tied herself next to him so that they could keep each other as steady as possible.

Someone yelled. Ruby looked up and saw the lookout

dangling by his rope from the crow's nest, but he managed to haul himself back up to it.

Tremendous waves loomed over the ship. Ruby could barely look as they crashed against Renegade—everyone was soaked to the bone and freezing. She shut her eyes tight, sending silent hopes that they would all survive this.

She was starting to think they wouldn't.

THE CELEBRATION

*I*t took everything inside of Ruby to keep herself on her feet. She hit her head a few times and scraped her arms and legs against the rough pieces of wood on the side of the ship. She was shaking, both from the cold and the effort it took to survive the storm's onslaught.

"Ruby!" Dirk yelled, steadying her after a particularly hard fall. "Are you okay?" All she could do was nod. "We'll get through this! You didn't come this far just to die now, understand?" Again, she just nodded.

She didn't know what she would have done if she didn't have Dirk. He truly deserved the world.

Another wave rolled over the ship. Ruby held her breath and was yanked backwards, but miraculously, the ship surfaced again. Ruby spluttered. Salt water burned inside of her nose.

After what felt like an eternity, the waves began to calm. The waters were still rough, but they weren't threatening, especially after what the main part of the storm had been like.

A rogue wave crashed hard into the port side of the ship,

just as Ruby was about to untie herself, and the pouch went flying over the edge. It had been weathered enough that the leather had started to break apart, and Ruby watched, horrified, as it disappeared beneath the waves.

She pulled the end of the rope and ran after it, diving into the water without even thinking. She couldn't see anything in the dark water, but she felt the pouch graze the edge of her fingertips.

She grabbed it and found that the dragon scales had spilled out of it.

She kicked harder even as her lungs were crushed by the heavier weight of the water above her. Her ears felt like they were going to burst, and she searched helplessly for the dragon scales as her consciousness started to fade away.

Somewhere above her, a warped splash sounded. She kept swimming, trying to get to the scales, but someone yanked her away, just as a veil of black took over her vision.

The next thing she remembered was coughing up sea water and clutching her ears, swaying as her hands came away bloody. Someone was shouting at her, but her vision was fuzzy, and it was too bright to make anything out. Her chest ached. She was breathing hard, trying to take in as much air as she could, and her whole body trembled with cold and exhaustion.

"Are you insane?" someone yelled. Ruby thought it had only been moments later, but when her eyes adjusted, she wasn't in the bright sun anymore—she was belowdecks. Dirk's worried face floated above hers, and in seconds, she sunk into the blackness again.

This was how it was for a long time—fading in and out of consciousness. Sometimes, she caught only glimpses of the commotion going on around her. Other times, she could understand the soft voices that spoke.

Finally, when she managed to stay conscious, she found

Dirk hovering over her, tucking her hair behind her ears. She was wrapped in blankets, but she still shivered violently. Her stomach was painfully empty, and she felt queasy.

"Water," she rasped, and Dirk called for someone else. A crew member Ruby didn't recognize brought a wooden cup, and she drank the fresh water quickly. Still, it gave her flashbacks to nearly drowning in the sea.

"I can't believe you risked your life for a few scales," Dirk said softly. Ruby gasped, and Dirk shook his head. "No, we didn't find them."

"We have to." Ruby tried to sit up and leave her bed, but Dirk gently pushed her back down.

"We can't. There isn't time to go back. We've already docked, and Woodruff knows we lost the scales."

"I'm going to die," she said, looking into a distant corner of the room.

"Between me and Devereux, we convinced him that you killed the dragon. He came down here and saw you, which added to the lie—he believes you did everything you could to get the scales back as proof. He trusts Devereux, and in this case, that happened to work out in our favor."

"No, Woodruff would never believe that." Ruby weakly batted at his hands as she tried to sit up again.

"Check your head. Your headdress is gone."

Ruby moved her hands to her hair and realized that Dirk was right. There was no headache.

"Do you believe me now?"

"Yes," Ruby said, but she still couldn't understand why Woodruff would simply trust her, even if Devereux did lie for her. She was suddenly relieved that she'd made up with Devereux, because she had a feeling that he wouldn't have lied for her if he didn't deem her worthy of respect. "Can I please get up now?"

"Woodruff prepared a celebration for you," Dirk said as

he helped her to her feet. "He's so wrapped up in the idea of you being the perfect dragon slayer that he hasn't stopped to wonder if you would ever betray him."

"A celebration?" Ruby asked in shock. They went up the stairs and into the fresh air.

"I think it's more to celebrate the fact that the memory loss potion works, but to hide the true meaning behind it, he's calling for it in your honor—the hero who nearly died trying to prove herself. In his eyes, you're absolutely perfect, and he doesn't want to believe anything different."

"Ruby!" Devereux hurried towards her from where he was standing on the gangway. He pulled her into a strong hug that she didn't expect, but she hugged him back regardless. "You're a fool, you know that?"

"Do you respect fools?" Ruby asked, and Devereux laughed.

"Usually, no, but you are the exception," he said, pulling away quickly.

"Thank you for lying for me," Ruby said under her breath, and the captain gave an imperceptible nod

He and Dirk both helped her off the ship to where Woodruff, the king, and some of the king's guards were waiting.

"I hear you've done incredibly well on your quest!" Woodruff exclaimed, clapping his hands together. Ruby understood what Dirk meant—it was all in his eyes, the excitement, the pride that he had found someone to do all of the dirty work for him.

"I killed the dragon," Ruby said, "and lost the scales in a storm in my effort to get back to the kingdom before your headdress could kill me."

Woodruff flinched and glanced over at Devereux. "Well, how wonderful that it all worked out! Come, I'm sure Dirk has told you that there will be a celebration for you tonight. You will be readied by the palace's maids."

Ruby was ushered away by Woodruff. Dirk and Devereux followed behind, and the king took his time in catching up. "Are they coming to the celebration?" Ruby asked, trying to slow down so that she could walk closer to Dirk and Devereux.

"Dirk is, of course. As for Devereux, I'm sure he has other places on the sea to be."

"I don't know, I think I could manage to stick around. You know how I love parties, Woodruff."

Woodruff grimaced— he didn't seem to realize that Devereux had come with them.

Woodruff brought the group into the palace. Devereux and Dirk were sent into the same room to be pampered and dressed for the celebration. Woodruff started to lead Ruby away, but she stopped. "Would it be possible to be near them?" she asked Woodruff innocently. "I don't know the palace very well, and I would feel much more comfortable if I had a room by my squire." Then, she leaned in and whispered, "I don't know if I trust that Devereux character all that much. I want to make sure that Dirk is alright."

Woodruff didn't seem to trust Ruby at first, but at the mention of her being wary of Devereux, he nodded agreeably. "He is a very wily pirate. I wouldn't want him stealing, either. Very well, you may have this room." He gestured to the room right next door.

It was huge, far bigger than Ruby needed it to be and different from the last room she'd been in. There were white walls and a small line of windows that went around the entire room at eye level. The huge bed was on a raised platform that had little steps leading up to it. There was a luxurious bathroom with a wardrobe just outside.

"I will fetch your maids, stay put." Woodruff looked reluctant to leave Ruby alone, but he did. She waited as his foot-steps retreated outside the door, then quickly left to check on Dirk.

A woman dressed in white opened it. "Who are you?"

"Ruby," she said, "the dragon slayer."

"You cannot be in here at the moment, Ruby. The boys are getting ready for the celebration." The woman shut the door, and Ruby returned to her own room.

She had a feeling that Woodruff planned on keeping them separated until he could keep an eye on all of them, and he was right to. Ruby felt like there was so much to discuss with Dirk and Devereux, like finding a way to not drink the potion without Woodruff noticing. She was terrified that everything would fall apart, and she would be forced to forget again, or worse, that Woodruff would catch on and kill her.

Every moment he was gone, she worried that what the younger dragon slayer had said was true— that Woodruff could sense when a dragon wasn't really dead. If that was the case, though, surely he would have confronted her immediately after she had spared the dragon on the mountain? Why would he have drawn out the lie even further?

Ruby's door burst open. Three women dressed similarly to the one that had answered the door in the other room bustled in. Immediately, they discussed what to do with Ruby. One of them rolled in an open wardrobe with colorful dresses inside of it.

Ruby was herded into the bathroom and was undressed before she could even tell the women that she could wash herself. One of the women poured steaming water into the bathtub, and Ruby flinched as she was gently pressed down into it. Her head was submerged for a moment, and she came up sputtering.

"Oh, it's not that hot," one of the women chuckled kindly. "Are you alright, dear?"

"Fine," Ruby panted, but the memory of drowning had come pounding back into her mind. "Sorry," she said, when she noticed she'd splashed them.

"Not to worry," the same woman said. "Forgive me— we've been rude. I am Angelina." She bobbed a curtsy.

"Meridian," the maid with dark, curly hair announced, also curtsying.

"The silent one's Ayleen," Angelina said, nodding her head at a taller woman with bright green eyes.

"We were told you killed a dragon," Meridian confessed quietly. She was working on Ruby's scalp, massaging some sort of soap into it, while the other two scrubbed every inch of Ruby's body. "What was it like?"

"Yes," Ruby said. "It was beautiful in a powerful sort of way. It was giant and white. It spoke to me through dreams."

"What did it say?"

"Meridian, you're prying." Angelina snapped.

"Sorry."

"No, it's alright." Ruby closed her eyes and relaxed. She didn't know it was possible to feel so good. "It warned me that if I wanted to end its life, it would end me first," she lied. "That's all."

"Wow," Meridian gasped.

The women were quiet after that. After Ruby was so clean that she felt as if she should sparkle, they pulled her out of the bath and wrapped her in a towel. Ruby's hair took a long time to dry, but the women worked quickly, styling it in soft, elegant waves.

As soon as they had finished, they started putting all manner of products on Ruby's face. She felt uncomfortable, but when she looked in the mirror, she was pleasantly surprised by how different she looked.

Her cheeks were the slightest bit rosier. Her eyelids and eyelashes were darker, and her skin looked flawless. Her lips were painted a sultry red, and she sucked in a breath, blinking at the person in the mirror.

"Do you like it?" Meridian asked. She'd done most of the work. "We thought a simple look was best, since we don't know which dress you'll pick."

"I love it," Ruby said, though she couldn't imagine that this was simple. She raised a hand to touch her skin, but Angelina batted it away.

"No touching!" she snapped before pulling Ruby to her feet. "Makeup is delicate. It comes off easily, and we don't want you to look like a mess at the celebration."

"Sorry," Ruby murmured. Angelina held out a hand for Ruby's towel, and she felt exposed again. She shivered while Ayleen went through the wardrobe.

"She's really good at choosing the right color and the right size," Meridian murmured from behind Ruby. "Watch."

Meridian was right—Ayleen chose a beautiful, midnight blue dress with ruffles that flowed down from the chest to the ground. She carefully eased it over Ruby's head, and when Ruby looked in the wardrobe's mirror, she almost didn't recognize herself.

The dress's straps slipped off her shoulders, and she tried to push them up, only stopping when Meridian told her that they were supposed to be like that. The waist was tight but bearable. It wasn't as heavy as her armor, but she felt awkward walking around in it. She was thankful when Ayleen chose flat shoes from the bottom of the wardrobe rather than one of the ones that towered off the ground and looked impossible to walk in.

The final touch was fixing up Ruby's hair. Ayleen brought back pieces from either side of Ruby's face and braided them, as well as separating a section at the back of her head before braiding all three braids together.

"You've all been incredible," Ruby said when Angelina and Meridian stood there awkwardly.

"You'll blow everyone away at the celebration," Meridian smiled. "I just know it."

Ruby gave her an answering smile. A knock sounded at her door, and she answered to see that Devereux and Dirk stood before her, polished and dapper.

Neither of them made a sound, and she fidgeted uncomfortably.

"Wow," Devereux finally said, and Dirk shot him a cutting glance. "What?"

"Nothing," Dirk muttered, shaking his head. He offered Ruby his arm, and she took it. "You look amazing."

"I feel strange." Ruby tried to push up one of her sleeves again. Devereux stopped and went around to her other side, and he offered her his arm as well. "How am I supposed to not drink the potion without Woodruff noticing?" she breathed. No one was around as the two men led her to wherever the celebration was taking place. All of the hallways looked the same to her, and she was impressed they knew where to go.

"I'll cause a distraction," Devereux answered. "Woodruff hates when he isn't in control. If he makes you drink the potion at the celebration, which I expect he will, I'll start something so that his attention is drawn away."

Ruby nodded. Dirk started to say something, but he stopped when footsteps sounded from around the corner.

It was Woodruff.

"Ah, I was just coming to fetch you three!" he beamed. Ruby could see the barest hint of anger that they'd had a few moments alone, and she knew Devereux was right about

Woodruff always needing to be in control. "You all look marvelous."

"So do you, Woodruff," Ruby said kindly.

"Come, let's get you to your celebration!" Woodruff gestured towards the ornate doors that were open in front of them.

Ruby took a deep breath and stepped forward.

MOST SUCCESSFUL OF THEM ALL

*T*he celebration was lavish.

The floor was smooth and polished beneath her feet, and it gleamed a rich gold. A brilliant chandelier hung in the middle of the giant room, spiraling down with crystals dripping off it. Beneath it, a silver fountain burbled merrily as crystal clear water spouted out of it and landed in elegant pools. Tables were set up beneath giant windows that were accentuated with flowing banners. A luxurious spread of food was set out, and guests milled about, laughing and dancing to the faint strains of the string quartet that played to the side.

"What do you think?" Woodruff asked, guiding her over to one of the tables. Dirk and Devereux stayed on either side of her the entire time, and Ruby assumed Woodruff didn't like that at all.

"It's wonderful," she admitted. That was the truth—it really was wonderful—but it also seemed excessively opulent. She'd thought she would be the fanciest one there with her makeup, but plenty of other women, and even men, were dressed in impressive displays of what could only be the latest fashion. Some had patterns delicately painted on their cheeks: ombre swirls, scales, and even wispy flowers, all of which were matched perfectly with the colors on their eyelids.

"I'm glad to hear it." Woodruff casually picked up a chalice that was sitting on the table, but Ruby recognized the purple liquid inside of it immediately. "A drink?" he asked, holding it in front of Ruby.

"No, thank you," Ruby said politely, looking around. "I'm not thirsty."

Woodruff held the chalice for a long moment. Ruby worried he would tell her that it would give her all of her memories back, and then she would have no excuse. Instead, Woodruff put it back on the table. She didn't miss the glance he exchanged with the man behind it who was dressed in servant's clothes.

"Well, how about a dance, then?" Woodruff asked, offering his hand to Ruby.

"Oh, I don't know how to dance," she demurred, clinging to Devereux and Dirk, who had stayed silent the entire time.

"I'll show you!"

"She isn't interested," Dirk said, cutting in.

"It's just one dance," Woodruff gritted out. "Ruby doesn't need you making decisions for her, Dirk."

"Devereux!" Melody approached the group and pulled him away.

"It's okay," Ruby said, turning to Dirk. He reluctantly let go of her, and Woodruff led Ruby out into the center of the room.

He twirled her and led most of the dance, and Ruby was surprised to find that she could keep up.

"You seem like you know how to dance," Woodruff commented. This was the first time Ruby had ever seen the man this happy.

"Maybe I do. If only I had my memories," Ruby said pointedly. She didn't want to coax him into giving her that chalice, but if she didn't start asking for her memories, he would suspect something was wrong.

"If only." Woodruff grinned. "Don't worry; you have completed your mission, and you will have them back by the end of the night. I must say, I couldn't be more proud of you."

"I thought you would be angry with me when I returned, for how I treated you before I left."

"Oh, no. Don't worry, that's all in the past. All that matters to me is success, and you, my dear, have been the most successful of them all."

They were quiet for the rest of the dance. A few of the other guests gave her surreptitious glances, and she couldn't tell what any of them meant.

When the song ended, Woodruff pulled Ruby enthusiastically away to where the musicians had been playing on a risen platform. He jumped up on the podium, startling some of them, and he pulled Ruby up beside him.

"Attention!" he called, picking up a half-finished glass from a side table in front of the platform. He clinked a fork against it, and the clear sound rang throughout the room. Everyone went quiet. Ruby desperately searched the crowds for Dirk and Devereux. "We are holding this celebration in honor of a very special guest! May I present Ruby, the dragon slayer! She has traveled to the islands and has killed the most powerful dragon this kingdom knows of. He is no longer a threat to us, because of this young woman's bravery!" Woodruff gripped her hand and raised it in the air while the guests cheered.

"Can we get down now?" Ruby asked Woodruff quietly. One of the musicians snickered behind her.

"Not yet, my dear." He kept her hand firmly in his as the same man from before approached them with a silver platter that held two chalices. Woodruff finally let go of her hand and leaned down to pick them both up.

"A toast!" Woodruff smoothly handed her one of the chalices.

Ruby was frozen. With all eyes on her, it would be impossible for her to avoid drinking the potion.

Her heartbeat thundered in her ears, and she lifted the chalice to her lips. Maybe she could simply hold it in her mouth and rush off to the bathroom, or she could throw it all up. She was afraid, and drinking from the chalice was the thing she least wanted to do, but it was looking like she wouldn't have a choice.

Then, the sound of swords clanging against each other tore her attention away from the potion. She lowered the chalice in relief and watched as Devereux and Dirk sparred across the floor.

"She doesn't deserve you!" Dirk called loudly, letting Devereux push him back towards the fountain.

"Stop this madness!" Woodruff yelled, unwilling to take his eyes off Ruby. Still, with a frustrated sigh, he stepped down from the platform. Ruby followed closely behind, easing over to his side next to where a giant potted plant obscured her from most of the crowd.

"What makes you think she deserves you, squire? You'll never be anything more than that!" Devereux snarled convincingly as he pushed Dirk back to the fountain. Ruby realized they were arguing over her, and she smiled internally at their antics. They had really saved her this time.

The loud sounds of steel against steel masked the fact that they were getting closer and closer to the fountain. Dirk easily jumped up into one of the higher pools, and he gripped the bottom portion of the chandelier, ready to swing down from the fountain. Woodruff's eyes had gone as wide as saucers, and when he looked back at her, she mimed taking a long drink of the potion in the chalice. Seemingly satisfied, Woodruff turned his gaze at the dueling pair.

As soon as his back was turned, Ruby emptied her chalice into the plant. She hoped the musicians behind her hadn't seen her do it, but they had no reason to report it to Woodruff if they had.

He broke up the fake fight, though Devereux and Dirk still kept up their scowls.

"No swords in the ballroom!" Woodruff yelled as he angrily ushered both of the men towards the door. Ruby hurried after them.

"What was that about?" she demanded, putting an irritated expression on her face. "Why would you cause a commotion during a celebration meant for me? I should have known you were no more than a pirate," she accused Devereux, ignoring the twinge of guilt rising up in her before turning to Dirk, "and you! If you want to be a knight, this is no way to behave!"

Woodruff turned to look at her in surprise, and she brought her chalice to her lips and mocked taking the last drink.

Once the men were through the door and left to wait outside the ballroom, he turned to her with a slight smirk on his lips. "You didn't need to scold them, Ruby, but I'm sure they've learned their lesson. I'm sorry your special moment was interrupted."

"Don't worry," Ruby acted as if she was stifling a yawn against the back of her hand. "The drink was wonderful, though I'm feeling very tired."

"It would be a shame to leave your own celebration so early, but I understand. Let's get you back to your room, how does that sound?"

"Perfect," Ruby favored him with a sleepy smile, allowing Woodruff to lead her past Dirk and Devereux. She glanced back at them as she was helped away, and to her surprise, they both had genuine anger in their expressions, though she didn't know if the anger was directed at each other or at her. She had been rather harsh on both of them. She made a mental note to apologize later and realized she would finally get to keep her memories.

Ruby feigned drowsiness and leaned on Woodruff more and more as they got closer to where she was staying. He opened the door and escorted her to the bed. The moment Ruby laid down in it, she shut her eyes and pretended she was already in a deep asleep.

She felt Woodruff's presence remain at the foot of her bed.

"Guards!" he called after a moment of watching her. Two men dressed in full suits of armor entered. "Take her to the dungeon—the same one she was in last time, that one should be empty."

"Yes sir, but the dungeon isn't empty. Reveland was moved to the cell at the very end after he had another one of his violent fits."

Woodruff was silent for a moment. "That's fine, just put her in the same cell as usual. I just don't want Ruby anywhere near him, understand? Make sure they don't talk."

Ruby realized Reveland must have been the man with purple eyes, the other dragon slayer. Ruby felt the guards lift her body and carry her. It took conscious effort to stay limp, and Ruby opened one of her eyes to pay attention to the passageways they were taking so that she would know where to go after she got out of her cell.

The familiar stench of the dungeon greeted her. She was carried down the same steps as before, except this time, she knew it. Her old cell door creaked open, and she was laid on a hard cot.

Woodruff had followed them down. "Good," he

murmured to himself, though there seemed to be a little bit of sadness in his voice. "I'll return for you in the morning, precious dragon slayer."

His footsteps, along with the guards', retreated from the dungeon. Ruby didn't open her eyes until everything was perfectly quiet, and she crawled up to the bars to look down at the other end. She wanted to speak to Reveland, but she was afraid that someone would hear her, and she would be caught in her lie. She couldn't risk it.

Ruby decided to bide her time and be patient—she had to be when there was nothing to do in her cell except think— but she was anxious to escape. A part of her hoped that Dirk and Devereux would come for her, but another part of her hoped that they wouldn't do anything rash. Perhaps Reveland would try to speak to her. But unfortunately, as the night stretched on, all remained quiet.

Ruby figured that it would be best to get some sleep. After all, she knew she would have a long day tomorrow.

A VERY LONG DAY AHEAD

*D*espite feeling drained, Ruby stayed awake. Knowing what tomorrow would bring made her too anxious to sleep—it felt like there was too much to figure out, like how she would get away from what she would have to do. She'd told herself that her priority should have been saving dragons, which meant going along with Woodruff's plan, but now, it didn't feel like enough. Woodruff had to be stopped.

IN A FUTILE ATTEMPT TO fall asleep, she found herself imagining a life with Dirk after all of this, a life away from the endless darkness. But as the hours dragged on, all she could see was Woodruff's face twisted in an evil sneer.

He would make her fight another half-orc tomorrow, and Ruby would have to convince him that she didn't remember anything. There was too much that could go wrong. She wanted to recruit the half-orc rather than kill him, but to do that, she would have to find a way to get to him. It would be risky, since she was sure that the half-orc would want nothing more than to kill her, but she had to try.

That would only be the first step. Everything else would be in fate's hands. Without knowing how her battle with the half-orc would end, it would be impossible to know what would happen next.

Sleep didn't come for a long while yet, but her dreams were plagued with her worries. She tossed and turned all night, sleeping for what felt like minutes at a time. The last time she woke, Woodruff stood imperiously outside of her cell.

"Good morning, dear," he said with a smile, a deceptively kind expression on his face. The smell of food drew Ruby's attention to the floor of the cell, where one of Woodruff's henchmen had set a bowl down. "My name is Woodruff, and you had better eat up. You are going to have a very long day ahead of you."

GOOD AT KILLING

*W*oodruff explained everything in the exact same way he had before. Ruby answered all of his questions with some of her natural sass, and he seemed pleased that she seemed the same as before.

He told her how she supposedly murdered someone in the king's court, how she suffered a concussion and lost all of her memories, how her punishment would be death…and Ruby listened silently.

Suddenly, Woodruff stopped his lengthy explanation and gave her a searching look.

"Why are you looking at me like that?" Ruby demanded angrily.

"Does death not concern you?" Woodruff inquired.

Ruby shrugged carelessly, playing off her misstep. "I suppose I'm just shocked, is all," she allowed some sadness into her voice as she stared down at the ground. "I don't know what to say to that. What should people say when they learn that they're going to die?"

"Well, you have a chance to fight for your freedom," Woodruff smiled again. Almost all of his initial concern had disappeared, and he went on to tell her about the half-orc. She made a point to refer to him as an orc, which both angered and pleased Woodruff as it usually did.

"Will I have any help at all?" she asked, wanting the conversation to lead to Dirk. "When I survive, what will my next challenge be?"

"You will only have a weapon of your choice. As for your second quest, how I love your confidence! Unfortunately for you, I will say nothing of it until you've either won or died. Consider it motivation."

"I'm sure if you told me what the quest was, I'd be all the more motivated," she crossed her arms and stared at Woodruff.

She was disappointed when he still refused to tell her.

"Patience, child. I know you want to find out," he winked at her before retreating from her cell with his henchmen. Ruby grabbed the plate and ate the terrible-tasting food that was on it. One of the henchmen had also left her water, and she thirstily gulped the entire bowl down.

Her hope had been to find a way to meet Dirk before the first challenge took place, to tell him what she was planning so that he could help her, but clearly, that wasn't going to happen.

As before, Woodruff told her she had some time to mentally prepare herself for the fight. But how was she supposed to be ready when she had so much time to stress over all of the small details?

Eventually, Woodruff returned. She stood before him dressed in a few pieces of light armor, and the guards took her to the weapons room, where she chose the spear and shield over the other weapons. She fell down into the arena and was swallowed by the sound of the crowds roaring around her. On cue, a half-orc lumbered out from a door on the other side of the arena.

He was enormous, far bigger than the last one Ruby had faced, with muscles bulging under his skin and gruesome, sharp tusks framing his mouth.

Ruby charged first, aiming her spear at him. She worried about making the fight seem real enough without hurting him too badly.

He slammed down his hammer, and Ruby skidded to the side. At the last moment, she wrapped her hand around the shaft of the hammer and was picked up along with it. She jumped onto the orc's shoulder and gave him a shallow slice with the tip of her spear while speaking quickly.

"I knew one of your brothers," she hissed, loud enough for the half-orc to hear but quiet enough so that no one else did. "We fought. He told me what the kingdom did to you."

The half-orc roared and shook her off. She landed on her back in a puff of dirt, and if the half-orc had slammed down his hammer as fast as he had before, she wouldn't have survived. He was the slightest bit slower, giving Ruby barely enough time to get out of the way. She charged at one of the half-orc's thick legs and spun her spear around so quickly that none in the crowd could see, jabbing him with the blunt end of her weapon. The half-orc seemed to catch on, letting out a convincing roar and smearing the blood from the wound on his shoulder onto his leg.

Ruby slowed herself a little bit, allowing the half-orc to pick her up and roar in her face. She pretended to struggle as the half-orc gripped her tighter. "I can help you get your revenge. Help me kill the humans. Let me win this, and I will only pretend to kill you, and you'll be dragged out as though you're dead. That's when you make your move."

The half-orc let Ruby slip through his fingers. She scuttled backwards, looking as though she was losing, and the half-orc chased her.

"How can I trust you? You're one of them," he growled as

he swatted at her, and Ruby felt the answering gust of wind propel her forward. She spun around and ran at the half-orc, burying the dull end of her spear in the ground and using that to leap up to the half-orc's shorts. She stabbed at him, but only barely touched the tip to his leg. He roared again. She could tell he wanted to trust her, but she understood why he was so unsure.

"If you kill me, they'll kill you anyways," Ruby said in a hushed whisper, remembering how Woodruff had saved her. "If I kill you, you die. Trust me when I say that I'll let you live. These humans have hurt me, too. They steal my memories and make me repeat the same quest over and over again, sending me into this arena to kill your kind and then out into the real world to slay dragons. I'm putting an end to it. None of your brothers will ever be forced in this arena again."

Throughout her talking, Ruby clambered up the half-orc's body to get to his head. He was swatting at her slowly, allowing her to get to where she was. She hesitated with her spear, waiting for the half-orc's answer.

"Okay," he finally agreed, and Ruby yelled out as though she was striking the killing blow. She stabbed the half-orc, drawing enough blood for the humans to believe he was dead, and the orc fell, lying motionless in the arena dirt.

Ruby vaulted off the orc's body and landed on the ground as the crowd cheered even louder. They were near where the half-orc had entered the arena, which made it convenient enough for the guards to take him. The only bit of worry left in Ruby was that she had killed the half-orc too quickly for Woodruff to believe it, but he couldn't voice that concern without confessing that he was the one taking her memories.

Ruby lifted her spear in victory, her face expressionless and covered in the half-orc's blood. Behind her, he groaned and took a last, shuddering breath. She turned to look at him.

He kept his eyes open, staring blankly at the ceiling of the arena. She hoped that he would be able to keep that up, and she dipped her head subtly at him as she turned back towards her exit point.

She hoped she would be able to find the half-orc again after this. Now that she'd won the first challenge, Dirk would be meeting her for her first time. She rolled her eyes internally. He could help her escape, and they, along with the half-orc, could get away.

"Well done!" Woodruff approached Ruby, though he didn't look as pleased as she'd hoped. "That was a rather quick battle."

"I guess I'm just good at killing," Ruby said, pressing her spear and shield into Woodruff's arms and walking right past him.

"Consider me impressed." Woodruff followed her back up to where her armor was taken off and she was led, once more, back to her prison.

She tried to focus on the sounds, listening for any sign that the half-orc had started his attack, but there was no yelling or roaring. He was biding his time, and that was exactly what Ruby needed him to do.

She didn't get much of a chance to listen, because Woodruff started talking as soon as he had shut her in the cell again. "Have your memories started to return?"

"No," Ruby lied. "They're still just barely out of reach. It's like they're blocked off."

Woodruff tapped one of his fingers to his chin. "How very strange. I will research solutions that may require magic. Meanwhile, your next challenge is to return five dragon scales to us. We've located a dragon in the nearby mountain range that's been causing some trouble." Ruby's heart pounded faster. Did Woodruff know? Was he sending her to the same dragon she'd already killed?

"That sounds familiar," she murmured, even though she knew it was a risk. She turned and looked at Woodruff, her brows knitted in concentration. "Have I been there before?"

"I don't believe so, no," Woodruff said neutrally, though the corners of his mouth pulled down. He looked at her with mild suspicion.

"I DON'T KNOW what you did in your free time, and I doubt it was spent in the mountains. The place I'm sending you to is on the other side of them, through the pass and then to the east."

That didn't sound like where Ruby had gone. She nodded her head and disappeared into her mind, acting like she was trying to get her memories back.

A few minutes later, Woodruff's henchmen appeared with a chest of armor, and Woodruff started telling Ruby that she would be issued a squire. Ruby could barely contain her excitement. She was so close to getting away from this kingdom—her plan with the half-orc had worked, and she was sure he would cause plenty of ruckus, which would allow for Ruby and Dirk to make their escape.

"He should be arriving soon," Woodruff murmured, and Ruby started to worry, though she tried not to show it.

FOOTSTEPS POUNDED DOWN THE STEPS, and Dirk burst through the door, panting heavily. There were scratches all over his arms and his face. "Woodruff, we have an issue," he gasped. "The half-orc isn't dead! He's on a rampage!"

"What?" Woodruff wore a thunderous expression. He looked from Dirk to Ruby. "How did he not die?" he asked angrily, rattling the bars of her cell. Screams rang out from the direction of the steps.

"I thought I killed him!" Ruby cried. "Give me a weapon—I'll do it for good this time!"

Woodruff looked like he wanted time to think, but Dirk urged him to help the people, and Ruby urged him to let her leave.

He looked overwhelmed. "Both of you, stay here!" he snapped. "I'll deal with this!"

He and his henchmen ran up the stairs. Dirk looked at Ruby questioningly.

"You remember me, right?" he asked, looking as if he was afraid of the answer.

"I didn't drink it," Ruby promised, and Dirk hugged her quickly.

"Come on, let's get your armor on," Dirk said, putting it on her faster than she could have done it herself. He had also managed to bring her spear. Woodruff had left it near the arena, and one of the guards had brought it to Dirk. "Are you ready?"

Ruby nodded. "Yes, but first, we have to free Reveland."

"Who?"

Ruby pointed to the other end of the dungeon. She pulled Dirk that way to his cell, and the strange dragon slayer was crouched in the corner. He looked up with a wan smile on his face and no surprise in his eyes.

"We're here to free you," Ruby said. Dirk got to work with a new lock pick, and the lock clicked open. "Come on."

Reveland didn't move—he just stared at her, so Ruby went in and took his hand, trying to pull him to his feet.

"I have learned much," he said, an eerie quality to his voice, "including how fate and destiny are tied together. One is the end, and the other is the journey. It is not yet my time to leave, but I will see you again. That much I promise you."

Ruby looked at Dirk while Reveland bowed his head.

"We're leaving on a ship, if you change your mind," she said, leaving his cell door open.

She didn't have much time to think about that strange interaction before Dirk took her hand. He pulled her up the stairs and then down hallways Ruby couldn't differentiate from each other.

"Devereux is with his ship. He rushed in under claims to help put down the half-orc, but he's helping the half-orc. That was clever, Ruby, but incredibly stupid, because Woodruff's definitely onto you now."

"It's not like he can do anything about that while there's a half-orc raging through the palace halls!" Ruby called over the commotion.

People were running in every direction once they left the stairs. When she turned the corner, it wasn't the same half-orc that had pretended to die, but a different one. Ruby stopped in surprise. The half-orc roared.

"I'm on your side!" she yelled, holding her hands up. She lifted the part of her helmet that covered her face. "I am helping the one that set you free! Where is he?"

The half-orc paused as though he didn't trust her. A group of three soldiers came running, and Ruby and Dirk took them down. They hadn't thought the king's people would turn on them, so the first two were easy to kill. The third one fought back when she realized that Ruby and Dirk weren't on her side, and though she was strong, Ruby and Dirk overpowered her. She landed the killing blow to the woman's neck and looked back up at the half-orc.

Finally, he nodded. "Thank you," he rumbled. "My brother is in the courtyard."

"Good luck," Ruby said, dipping her head before following Dirk to the courtyard. She covered her face with her helmet again, and though she got looks from other guards that were racing towards the half-orc she was running from, no one attacked her.

They found the courtyard, and it was pure chaos. She hadn't realized that the kingdom had this many half-orcs. She found the one she'd battled. Devereux and Melody fought next to him.

"I'm so glad you could make it!" Devereux called sarcastically, taking down two guards at the same time.

Ruby pulled him and Melody away into a corner where they were safe as a new idea took place in her head. "We should free the dragons," she said. She looked from Devereux to Dirk. "Where does the kingdom keep them?"

Dirk looked at Devereux. "I never knew," he said.

Devereux's mouth was set in a grim line. "Follow me."

They ran out to the other side of the courtyard.

THE TIDES OF BATTLE

*D*evereuax led them through the palace, and they sprinted through the corridors.

"I'm impressed you still remember all of this," Ruby commented, panting as she tried to keep up.

"When you grow up in such a horrible place, you don't forget it." Devereux opened a door underneath a staircase in one of the main parts of the palace that looked just like the wall. The rest of them rushed through it, and Devereux followed behind them.

They went down a seemingly endless staircase, and the longer they walked, the narrow space became darker and darker.

"This is uncomfortable," Melody said, clutching onto her arms.

"We'll be back on open water before long," Devereux promised, looking back at her briefly. His voice echoed against the walls.

Eventually, they came to a hallway. Unlike the dungeon that Ruby had been in, this one was full of uneven rock, both below and on either side of them. Candles sat in candle holders to lead the way, but Ruby felt more comfortable just taking one with her.

Chains rattled ahead, where the hallway opened up into a giant room of the same terrain. Ruby saw massive outlines curled up. None of them were trying to escape.

"Woah," Dirk said quietly. He stopped to take it all in. "This is horrible. Do they just live like this?"

"Yes," Devereux answered, just as softly.

"I thought you said you fought for freedom," Ruby said to him. "If you knew about the dragons, you could have released them."

"I was here when they were working on memory loss potions. I was terrified that one would be used on me. When I discovered this place one day while running around the kingdom, that's what they held over me—the threat of taking my memories. That's part of the reason I went out to sea. I only play nice with Woodruff because that's what I've had to do to survive. You get that, don't you?" Devereux asked, looking over at Dirk.

Dirk nodded in understanding.

"I can't believe this," Melody said, walking forward. "So few dragons left in the wild, so many trapped down here." She approached a deep blue one. It looked at her and lifted part of its lip, growling low in its throat.

"Melody, be careful."

"It's a sea dragon." Melody knelt down next to it and put a gentle hand to its nose. It was angry at first, but then, it sniffed her hand and started to whine rather than growl. "It senses the ocean. We've got to free them all."

"I'm on it," Dirk said. He went to the first dragon, a pure white one that was much like the last one Ruby had encountered. All of them had metal muzzles that clamped their jaw closed. Chains held them down and kept their wings pressed to their bodies.

While Dirk started working on freeing them, Ruby sat down and crossed her legs. She closed her eyes and meditated, focusing on the raw power that filled this area to the brim.

Her vision was warped when she opened them again. It didn't take much effort to connect to the dragons that could speak to her through visions. Ruby could feel an air of desperation around them, but now, some stood in front of her, free and bowing their heads to her.

"We will help you in your fight against the corrupted one," a bright red dragon promised.

"Thank you," Ruby said. "We are working to free you, but only he has a lock pick." She nodded her head in Dirk's direction.

"Our muzzles can be loosened," a golden one said. "So can the chains on our wings. We know because the humans regularly tighten them, leaving horrible marks of pain across our bodies. If you loosen them enough, we can free ourselves and breathe our powers."

"We'll do that." Ruby paused. "Do any of you know anything about a purple-eyed dragon slayer named Reveland?"

The golden one dipped its head. "He was good to us. He tried to free us, as you have, but he was foolish. When the kingdom found out, he was brought down here. His hand was forced—he killed a dragon that was here once. At first, the kingdom believed that killing us would make Reveland want to slaughter even more dragons. And it did, but only for a short time. He started slaughtering us ruthlessly, but then, something inside of his soul crumbled. He couldn't bear to look at us. He broke and refused to kill us. He was wild. The connections between the dead dragons and the realms that he had severed caught up to him, so they pulled him away, thinking they could experiment on him."

The dragon paused, keen intelligence in its eyes. "If you know his name, he must be alive."

"He is. He's in a cell in the dungeon—I opened it for him and tried to get him to leave with us, but he said it was not yet his time."

The golden dragon tilted his head. He looked at the others in confusion, and they all stayed quiet.

"I did not think it possible," the dragon whispered. "One of the dragons he killed was known among us as Eselvia. She was one of the great ones, more powerful than most of us. She could see stars in the air, the breaths of life in the night sky, she told us. They all led to different paths one could take. It seems that Reveland may have that power, but this is not something to worry about now. I can hear the battle between the half-orcs and the humans. The half-orcs are sorely outnumbered, and many of them are dead. Free us, and we will turn the tides of battle."

"We will."

Ruby blinked, and she was back in her real body. Four dragons had been released.

"Go!" Ruby said, pointing to the stairs behind her. "The battle needs you." The dragons started running, and they burst through both the door and the wall. The entire room shook. "Some of the dragons told me that we can loosen their muzzles, and they can free themselves from there," Ruby told Devereux and Melody. They all ran to the remaining dragons and worked on the tight metal muzzles.

It was difficult, more strenuous than Ruby had expected. The metal creaked against itself as Ruby tried to turn the crank, and she was sweating by the time she had loosened two. Once they freed themselves, blasting ice or fire or air at the chains that still held them down, they helped the other dragons escape.

Soon enough, all of them were free. Ruby ran all the way

down the length of the room to make sure they hadn't missed one.

"Ruby, we have to get out of here!" Dirk called to her. She knew he was right—the ground was still shaking, and the room would collapse at any moment.

She followed after him, Devereux, and Melody as they ran for the broken door. She was exhausted, and her feet were sore, but the adrenaline pumping through her veins kept her on her feet. When they made it into the palace, everything was in shambles, and it was pure pandemonium.

It wasn't just the room—the entire palace was collapsing. Devereux and Melody led them away, but as they walked down a different corridor, they were confronted by yet another group of soldiers.

There was one for each person to fight. Ruby took the one with a ball and chain. It was difficult to avoid such a fast-moving weapon, so Ruby threw her spear, somehow managing to get it tangled in the thick chain. She charged at the guard, sending him to the ground as she ripped off his helmet. She punched him as hard as she could and took her spear back while he tried to recover. She finished him with a blow to the neck.

Melody had already won her battle by the time Ruby stood up. Dirk was fighting sloppily against a man with a staff, but he managed to break it and land the finishing blow. Devereux played cat and mouse with his opponent, jumping up on fallen columns and making his opponent run after him.

"Quit playing games," Melody panted.

"Where's the fun in that?" Devereux leaped over the man and stabbed him in the back.

"Let's go!" Ruby yelled.

"Let's hope that Renegade yet lives," Dirk said, and that got Devereux moving.

They raced out into the open air. Ruby looked up and was surprised when she realized that a few dragons were fighting other dragons.

"What is going on?" she demanded.

"Some of the dragons are so beaten by their handlers that nothing can motivate them to disobey," Devereux said sadly.

All of the obedient dragons had black or white markings on their bodies, marking them as belonging to the kingdom.

Ruby watched a free dragon dive at a kingdom one ruthlessly. Other free dragons tried not to kill kingdom dragons, and instead, tried to coax them to return to the wild, but Devereux was right—the kingdom dragons were beaten beyond repair.

"Watch out!" Dirk dove at Ruby, tackling her to the ground as a burst of fire scorched a line in front of them. Devereux and Melody were both safe, but the kingdom dragon opened its mouth again, a bright orange flame gathering at the back of its throat.

"I need you guys to cover me!" Ruby yelled, sitting down. She meditated, her focus on the kingdom dragons, and opened her eyes in the dream state.

All of the kingdom dragons looked at her, confused. Their real bodies were moving in extremely slow motion, but their dream ones were drawn to Ruby.

"You have a chance," she started, looking at each one's face. "You can kill your handlers and be free once more. Fight for the right side. I know they hurt you, and you fear they will hurt you again, but they won't. Nothing can stop you. Don't hurt those who simply want to help you."

Some of the dragons had too much fear within them to listen to Ruby when she came back to reality. They continued diving at the free dragons, and many were killed. The one that was about to attack Ruby's group again, though, tumbled out of the way at the last minute.

"Ruby, what are you doing?" Dirk screamed at her, pulling her to her feet. "Don't you dare disappear into your head right now!"

"I'm finished, look! That's why she moved out of the way! Stop, Devereux!" The pirate captain charged at the dragon, ready to kill her, but Ruby tackled him to the ground. "This one's on our side!"

The dragon got to her feet and turned her head, breathing a burst of fire on herself. It didn't scorch the dragon's scales, but it did get rid of the markings. She looked at Ruby and huffed an acknowledgement before taking off into the sky, finally free.

It broke Ruby's heart when the dragon was immediately attacked by another that was loyal to the kingdom. They fell towards the ground, and Ruby ran at them, trying to think of something she could do, but it was too late—the fire dragon died at the claws of a pure black one that Ruby hadn't seen in her dream state.

He turned on her and breathed acrid smoke that burned Ruby's nostrils and stung her eyes. She tried to listen and aim her spear, but it was no use.

A roar from another dragon sounded nearby. Ruby thought it was over, that this was her last moment alive, but another dragon's wings beat over her head, and a plume of fire shot straight towards the kingdom dragon.

When the smoke cleared, she saw an older fire dragon attacking the aggressive black one. The red dragon overshot, and it turned to breathe fire at the black dragon. Ruby practically dove at one of the palace walls, hitting her head against the hard stone. In that same moment, a grey kingdom dragon hurtled towards her and trapped her under the stone, making it impossible for her to breathe.

Her eyes stung, and she gasped for air. She tried to push the stone off, but it didn't move an inch.

"Ruby!" Dirk screamed, pushing through the battlefield. Devereux and Melody noticed. They all worked at pulling the stone away, but it was impossible. Ruby shook her head and tried to speak, only to find that she couldn't.

They didn't hear the grey dragon until it was nearly on top of them, but once more, the fire dragon intercepted its attack. After finishing off the black one, she dove at the grey one, killing it instantly with her fire. She scrabbled at the stone, freeing Ruby as the rest of them dove out of the way.

It didn't matter, because Ruby was blasted back by something else, an obsidian magic that bound her and slammed her into the wall. She turned and saw Woodruff, his eyes black with magic and anger.

The free dragons seemed to recognize him as their main torturer and started attacking him immediately. They should have been able to overpower him. They should have been strong enough, with their blasts of fire and ice and everything in between, but they weren't. Woodruff's black magic struck them through their chests and sent them spiraling into the ground.

Ruby fought against the shadows. They grew weaker as Woodruff used more power against the rest of the dragons, and eventually, she was able to break free. She raced to a red one that had just been shot down—Woodruff had missed her heart on purpose, leaving her to die a slow and painful death.

"I'm so sorry," Ruby whispered, falling to her knees and kneeling at the dragon's head. She laid a hand on the warm scales and stroked the side of the dragon's face, comforting her in the last moments she had before she faded. "Return to the endless skies."

The light died from the dragon's eyes, and she stared, unseeing. Her wings draped majestically over her body, and Ruby screamed in rage.

It was cut short by a shard of ice striking her hard in the

shoulder. She was pinned to the ground, unable to move. Pain lanced down her arm, but yet again, there was nothing she could do except stay put.

Devereux and Melody were desperately trying to fight off the other kingdom dragons, but there were too many. The free dragons were fleeing out into the skies, getting away from Woodruff while they still could, and Ruby held no resentment for them for doing so. She only wished that she was on their backs.

Ruby couldn't find Dirk, and that made her chest ache. Devereux and Melody were surrounded by walls of smoke, caught in place. Ruby looked to Woodruff. His attention was on the dragons that were flying away, and as she looked through the smoke, she could make out the outline of someone sneaking up on him with a sword.

It was Dirk. Ruby nearly shouted out of pure relief, but she stayed quiet as Dirk struck the man that had caused Ruby and many others so much misery throughout their lives. Woodruff grasped at the protruding blade and fell forward, shock on his face.

Ruby struggled harder to pull the icicle out of her so that she could see his dying moments up close, but she couldn't— it was too slippery.

All of Woodruff's dark magic fell away. Dirk turned from his motionless body and ran to Ruby, falling to his knees beside her.

"This will hurt," he whispered, tears in his eyes.

"Do it," she said, gritting her teeth as he pulled hard. Ruby howled in pain and clutched her shoulder with her opposite hand. Blood seeped between her fingers, and it felt like her shoulder had been ripped to shreds.

Dirk gathered her up towards his chest as kingdom dragons landed on the ground, and he held her as their worlds ended.

SENTENCED

*R*uby was thrown into a different cell, her arm dangling uselessly at her side. Dirk was chained across from her, with Devereux and Melody next to each of them. They were all chained to the ground the same way Reveland was.

"For the release of the kingdom's dragons, conspiracy against the kingdom, and the murder of Woodruff and many others, you are all sentenced to death," the female guard read from a scroll. All of them had been forced into simple black attire, and they had made sure to find Dirk's lock pick. "The execution will be public, and it will be held in one hour."

"Let me speak with the king!" Ruby tried to say. There was a gag in her mouth, but she mumbled around it anyway. "He would never allow this!"

Really, Ruby wanted to speak to the guard that had reminded her of Reveland's existence and helped her remember, but she figured that the easiest way to do that was to get to the king. Still, the guard shook her head. "You aren't getting anywhere near him," she stated coldly, before retreating from the dungeon.

Ruby looked over at Dirk. There was a heavy ache in her heart, and she already missed the sensation of him holding her as the kingdom dragons and their riders had closed in on them. She'd wanted to kiss him right then, but she was too flustered with everything that had happened.

She exchanged a glance with Melody. She couldn't see Devereux in the cell next to her, but she knew he had a similar look on his face as the rest of them did—a look of utter loss.

Time crawled by. Ruby could hear Reveland moving at the end of the dungeon. She couldn't help the frustration she felt that he didn't escape with them. Perhaps he could have changed the outcome, but something told her that he had a reason for staying behind, even if she didn't understand it yet.

But as the minutes ticked by, Ruby believed it less and less. There was no way that Reveland could save them. He was just as trapped as they were, though when the guards returned to keep an eye on them, a few of the guards regularly patrolled back to Reveland's cell.

There were two guards for each of them. Ruby's were rough as they yanked her hands and feet free and dragged her out of the cell, leaving her gag in place. She screamed in pain and swayed on her feet. The bleeding had stopped, but there was still a gaping hole in her shoulder that hadn't had time to heal. She couldn't move her arm at all.

Ruby tried to free herself from the grasp of the men, but it was hopeless.

Wriggling in the guards' hold and ignoring the burning pain in her shoulder, she managed to trip one of them as they went up the stairs, and he merely stumbled back into one of the guards behind her. Still, it gave Ruby a brief moment to run to Dirk and have him hold her one last time.

He did, tightly, and it was over too soon. Ruby was pulled

back and slapped hard across her cheek, but she barely registered it. The pain didn't even compare to her shoulder. The guard that had fallen cruelly wrenched her arm behind her back, and an agonized cry escaped from her lips as her knees buckled. Dirk screamed through his gag, but the guards didn't stop until Ruby stopped struggling.

She was out of strength. The guards had to support nearly all of her weight as she hung between them.

She could barely pay attention to where they were going, but she knew where they ended up—right where Woodruff had died.

There was a raised wooden platform with steps leading up to it, and at the top, four wooden blocks meant for the group's heads and arms stood empty. Around them, dragon bodies still lay as though to remind the prisoners of their failure. Devereux's ship bobbed peacefully in the distance, a sad reminder of their lost freedom.

Two men stood on the platform. One held an axe, and the other read from a scroll. In front of the platform, a crowd stood, whispering amongst themselves. When they saw the prisoners being led up to the blocks, a sudden hush fell over them.

Ruby was thrown towards the block, and her arms and head were pressed into the holes. Ruby was almost relieved that her pain would end. But when she imagined the cruel edge of the axe slicing through Dirk's neck, suddenly she wanted to cry from the sheer injustice.

She turned her head to look at him, and his soulful eyes looked back at her. He tried to move his lips around the crude gag, but he couldn't. Ruby couldn't understand what he wanted to say.

"For the murder of the nobleman, Woodruff, this group of rebels will be executed. They have brought chaos upon this kingdom, releasing dragons and plotting against our glorious kingdom. Today, that treachery ends. We will be rid of these heretics and schemers! Our kingdom will be safe once again. We will make examples of these rebels who have wronged us, so that others never will."

The executioner approached Ruby. She focused on the pain in her arm in an attempt to not worry about death, but it was impossible. It hung over her in the form of a blade, and she couldn't stop wondering what would happen after the axe fell. She had done horrible things, but she had also done some good. She was almost resigned to the fact that she wouldn't be able to live a life free of this place, but she had been loved by Dirk. She had learned the truth from him, and she was grateful for that. A single tear slipped down her cheek as the executioner prepared to strike.

"What is the meaning of this?"

The executioner paused mid-swing, and a collective gasp sounded as he turned and saw the king standing imperiously behind the crowd. Ruby released the breath she didn't know she had been holding and closed her eyes in relief.

"Your Majesty, they killed Woodruff and released dragons out into the sky," the man with the scroll said. His voice shook with quiet fury, and it was obvious he was displeased that they had been interrupted.

"My constable and I have come to some startling revelations...Woodruff was a scheming noble who killed my son!" There was heavy regret in the king's voice, and Ruby suddenly noticed Reveland at his side. "Woodruff kept these dragons in the palace without my knowledge, but I would have demanded their release long ago! Set these prisoners free immediately."

There was a long silence as they were freed of both the blocks and the gags. Dirk hurried to Ruby, tears staining his cheeks, and he gently pulled her to his chest, resting his chin on top of her head.

"I am so, terribly sorry for the things Woodruff has done to you," the king frowned, walking up the steps and onto the platform. He gestured towards Reveland, who was only a few paces behind him. "Reveland has opened my eyes. At first we thought he was just ranting nonsense, but finally I listened to him…and it was all true. We even planted him deeper in the dungeon to confirm his story."

Ruby dipped her head, still wrapped in Dirk's arms. "He was a terrible man."

"I was blinded like a fool. The experiments, the killing, I wish I had stood up to him. I knew of the half-orcs, but I never stopped him—his magic terrified me, and he was good at holding it over me. I will order the release of all the remaining dragons we currently hold captive, and I will make the necessary arrangements to prevent anything like this again, though I would not be surprised if you chose to leave. If you choose to stay, I would like to have your counsel in the future."

"At the moment, I would simply like some healing herbs," Ruby bit back a hiss of pain as she shifted to look at the terrible wound in her shoulder. If it wasn't cared for soon, she had a feeling that she wouldn't survive the blood loss.

"Of course, come with me."

The king led the way into the palace, and they followed, though Reveland stayed behind.

Ruby was given a room to rest in where healers looked after her. They tended to her arm constantly, first cleaning the wound and then closing it up with a bandage. The pain was excruciating, and she was exhausted, but at least she had some use of her arm back.

Dirk stayed with her through it all. Her bed was big enough so that they could lay in it together, and she became more and more relieved that she had lived. She couldn't imagine dying without experiencing a love like this.

"Dirk?" Ruby smiled as she looked at his relaxed expression.

His eyes fluttered open, and he started to sit up. "What's wrong? Is it your arm?"

Ruby shook her head and pulled him in for a tender kiss.

His lips were soft against hers. She tangled her good hand in his hair, and he held her gently, as though he was afraid of hurting her. When they pulled away from each other, Ruby could still feel his lips on hers.

"We should do that more often," Dirk said hoarsely, his lips still open as though he was in awe. His eyes flickered from Ruby's eyes to her lips, and her heart felt so full, she didn't know that such happiness existed.

Devereux and Melody stayed at the palace long enough to help the king free the rest of the dragons and to help them understand that they would never be hurt again. The particularly beaten-down ones required Ruby's attention, so she would meditate for hours to try to reach them. It was an incredibly difficult task, but she managed to get through to all of them.

The group stood on the sands with the king and Reveland to watch the dragons fly off into the sky...all but one. The iridescent green dragon looked at them curiously and tilted her head. This dragon had been one of the hardest to help.

"What is she doing?" the king asked in wonder.

"She wants us to leave with her," Ruby said. She looked to Devereux and Melody.

"I have my ship to get back to," Devereux cleared his throat, dipping his head. Melody nodded in agreement, and she darted forward, pulling Ruby into a strong hug

"I hope to see you both again," Melody said to them, smiling as she looked up at Devereux.

"Where will you be, now that you aren't working for the

king?" Ruby asked. The king had released them of their duties earlier in the day.

"I think we'll check out the islands for a while," Melody answered. Devereux looked surprised. "I think it's time I faced the truth of my people."

They turned and walked towards Renegade, and Ruby truly did hope to see them again. Then, she faced Reveland. "How did you know about Mara and Channing?"

"I killed a powerful dragon once," Reveland sighed, bowing his head. "I don't know how, but my body survived when her powers left her and expanded inside of me." His eyes seemed unfocused, as if he was peering into the past. "I should have died. I should have paid for what I did, but there was a reason she saved me—perhaps she thought I could provide the world something that she couldn't, and I intend to find out what that is. I will do right by her."

"Will you come with us?" Dirk asked.

Reveland shook his head. "My place is here, where I can help bring change to the world. Your place is among the dragons," he said cryptically, gesturing to the sea dragon that patiently waited for their decision.

"Thank you for all you've done." Ruby gave a respectful nod to Reveland and the king before taking Dirk's hand and approaching the sea dragon. She seemed nervous as they got on her back, and Ruby stroked a firm hand over her warm scales to calm her. The dragon pushed off the ground, and Ruby was unable to stop her peals of laughter as they soared freely through the air.

Flying was incredible. The wind whipped Ruby's hair in the wind, and she closed her eyes, relishing the chill of the air against her cheeks and the heat of Dirk's body at her back. She'd thought that everything would be smaller from the sky, but the ocean was just as wild and infinite as it had always been.

The dragon dove under the waves and resurfaced in a spray of sea water. Ruby and Dirk clung onto her scales tightly, laughing at the enthusiastic way the dragon swam. She spiraled through the water gracefully and dove underneath Devereux's ship, which was still docked. She emerged and landed right in the middle of the deck, sending a few of Devereux's men scuttling to the sides.

"Come on," Ruby laid a hand on the dragon's neck, "don't you want to be free?"

The dragon laid down in response. Devereux and Melody approached with wide smiles on their faces.

"Looks like we're sticking together," Ruby grinned as the dragon seemed to huff in agreement.

Renegade set sail, and the sea dragon took to the skies, circling the ship as they sailed for the horizon.

THANK YOU

I hope you enjoyed my novel! I have one favor to ask, could you please leave a review on either Amazon or Goodreads? Reviews help new authors such as myself more than you could ever imagine. When people are looking for a new read they check out the positive reviews. By leaving a positive review you'll help more people get to enjoy my books.

—J E Thompson

ABOUT THE AUTHOR

You know those kids who live in the pale blue light of their computer monitors? Well, J. E. Thompson was one of those youngsters. His childhood was spent obsessing over warlocks and bonus points, tirelessly questing to defeat the threats in his crumbling virtual empires, and above all, creating worlds and adventures for himself and his friends to enjoy.

But that scrawny swashbuckler has long since grown up, and these days, instead of planning out Dungeons and Dragons campaigns, J. E. Thompson is a software developer who has worked for some of the industry's top players, like the legendary Rockstar Games.

As a fiction author, he has written a fantasy adventure series titled The White Chronicles, which follows a cocky human warlock with a penchant for trouble. When he isn't dreaming up new adventures, J. E. Thompson is enjoying a quiet life in South Carolina with his wife and poodle.

For more information:
hello@jetwrites.com

CPSIA information can be obtained
at www.ICGtesting.com
Printed in the USA
BVHW080351040222
627977BV00010B/339